CW00865705

Cats Alone

By K.M. Leonard

For my brother, Patrick, and all of his amazing but sometimes insane ideas.

Chapter One

Hey. I'm Shadow, the leader of the End House Cat Tribe. You won't know me, but I'm pretty important to my Tribe, and my owner too. Joseph is his name. He's sitting here now, in the rubbish filled living-room, lounging in his usual ripped armchair, in front of the same battered T.V. My house-mates - Sophia, Sapphire and Ruby are curled up on the armchair with him, as am I. I command the top of the arm-chair, while Sapphire and Ruby - the Twins - take over the two arms. That leaves Sophia, a young, snow white kitten with a heart of gold, to curl up in Joseph's lap.

Joseph is a wrinkled old man, who cares for us cats like his own children. He has a little wispy white hair atop his wrinkled head, and his usually squinted brown eyes will only ever leave the T.V screen for us, literally. All he does is: shuffle to the kitchen and back; lie in his armchair; sleep for several hours on end; and, of course, occasionally go out for a few hours and come back with more junk, and cat-food. Every room is piled high with rubbish, and it stinks, but we get used to it. We made our beds from the tattered blankets and squashed cardboard boxes we found long ago, buried underneath the heaps of trash we have grown accustomed to. My bed, for example, is a cardboard box lined with bits of fabric and material, and the odd blanket, while the Twins have a fortress, made by stacking up tin upon tin of cat-food and filling the inside with rugs, blankets and old clothes.

At this moment in time, we are all in our designated spots on the armchair, watching some T.V show about cooking. This seems to remind old Joseph that we need to eat, as he slowly gets up, placing Sophie gently on the floor, and shuffles into the kitchen, wading through the mountains of rubbish, and the rattle of a tin opener tells us dinner is near. I meow, and we all scamper to the kitchen, scrambling over the rubbish then sliding down again, to see Joseph opening one of the many metallic grey tins of cat-food and pouring it out into three bowls (The Twins share a bowl). It tastes the same as always: just better than rats and mice but not as nice as a good bit of pigeon.

He pats me on the head with a shaking hand, before struggling with a rusty old tap, finally turning it on. Nothing. Not a drop of water comes out. Shaking his head, and muttering incomprehensible words, he pulls two buckets from the corner of the room to the window. It creaks and groans, but Joseph finally gets it open. He brings in two buckets filled with rain water, and puts out the two empty ones, before shutting the window and turning back to us.

By this time, we have finished eating and are looking at him curiously. He picks up each of our licked-clean bowls and fills them with water, his hand as precariously shaky as ever, before leaving us to drink. Threatening growls and rough barks fill the small house, as Joesph carefully opens a door to the left slightly, and a huge black nose comes poking out, slathering teeth clearly visible. This creature is a dog; a Staffordshire Bull Terrier to be exact, and certainly not counted as one of my Tribe.

We cats have only ever seen the beast once, and that was the day it arrived. A panting mess of white fur, straining at a chain lead, with a single brown spot over one eye. Joseph was yelling at it, something like 'Baxter!', so we presumed that was its name. But any attempts at talking proved useless, as it was shut in a small room and never came out. It still doesn't.

Anyway, Joseph picks up a strip of meat and throws it into the room, before slamming the door and locking it. The sounds of frenzied ripping and tearing tell us that the dog is enjoying and destroying its meal, so we finish our water before following Joseph back over the mountains of junk and into the living room, climbing into our places and continuing to watch T.V.

At this point, you may want to know what everyone looks like. Well, I'm Shadow, so, as you may have already guessed, my coat is inky black all over. As the leader of my Tribe and the only male - besides the dog and Joseph - in the house, I am also the tallest cat. The twins are next, Sapphire and Ruby. Sapphire is meek but smart and very shy, while Ruby is loud, brave and, unfortunately for us, has a very short temper. They are identical Twins, which means they are mirror opposites of each other. Ruby has one white foot, her front left, while on Sapphire it is her front right foot. Also, they both have a white spot on the very end of their tails. The main colour for both of their coats is ginger, of the brightest kind, and they share the same amber eyes.

Sophia, as I have already mentioned, is a

fully snow white kitten, with two innocent blue eyes. Me? I have grass green eyes, no markings anywhere, and, people say, a responsible and mature manner of doing things.

Joseph, after a few hours of being settled in front of the T.V, gets up and goes to the front door, still muttering words to himself. He leaves, only just getting the door open, and we are left alone.

"Finally!" Ruby sighs and settles herself on the armchair. "I thought we'd have to watch all of that awful football match."

"It wasn't too bad." I yawn and curl up on the top of the armchair.

"What do you think he's getting?" Sophia asked in her mild voice.

"Cat-food, more junk, another dog," Ruby starts flicking her tail in a bored manner as she talks, "Who knows?"

"Let's hope its not another dog. We don't need another Baxter." I say, shuddering at the thought, before I see Sophia shivering.

I take this as a sign that she's cold, and scan the rubbish for a blanket. Seeing one peeking out from under the Armchair, I leap down, land safely, grab it with my teeth and drag it over to where Sophia is sitting. I jump up onto the Armchair and cover her with it, before resuming my conversation with Ruby.

"If it is another dog, then I hope it's not as energetic as Baxter." Ruby says, scratching the Armchair absent-mindedly.

"It won't be. Old Joseph won't be able to deal with another dog like Baxter." I reply. "And anyway, who says he's getting a dog?"

"Sapphire says. She hears him when he mumbles, remember?"

I remember alright. Sapphire, by far the quietest cat that ever lived, is the closest to Joseph, and can always tell what he's saying when he is talking to himself. I'm sure he has a special place in his heart for her, but her entire heart is for him, and Ruby of course. Conversations in this house are either between me and Ruby or Sapphire and Ruby, with Ruby doing most of the talking. We don't generally get many words out of Sophia, except the odd 'thank you' when we do things for her.

"What exactly did she hear?" I ask, curious.

"She told me," Ruby rolls over and looks me in the eye, "That he said: 'Need a new blasted dog, old one too energetic, animal shelter will do, also need cat-food'."

" 'Also need cat-food'? Are you sure?"

"Positive. Does Sapphire ever lie?"

Thinking about it, I shake my head, and Ruby rolls back to her original spot. Sapphire is also on the Armchair, and I'm sure she's been listening to the entire conversation. Looking at her, I see her suddenly freeze up, and wonder what on earth is wrong. Her tails stops its usual calm swaying and her eyes are focused on one point. Slowly, I turn my head to see what she's looking at, then realise: it's a rat. I subconsciously lick my lips, before remembering that Sapphire is an expert mouser, and just as good at catching rats, as well as always sharing, so I decide to just watch.

She, ever so slowly, lifts herself up and prepares to pounce. The rat is still merrily nibbling away on a bit of old food, blissfully unaware of Sapphire's hungry eyes watching its every move. As soon as she is ready, she pounces. And you've never seen a cat pounce like Sapphire does. She launches herself at whatever is unlucky enough to be her prey, and never misses. Ever. This time, she catches the rat with her front two paws, killing it with a clean swat to the head, then picking it up and bringing it back to us. Oh yes, this rat was on the other side of the room, please remember.

"That's my Sapphire!" Ruby smiles, as Sapphire splits the rat between us and gives Sophia the largest bit.

The day then continues, with me and Ruby talking for several hours, before the sound of a door opening and shutting tells us that Joseph is home. But the pattering of feet in the hall tells us that he's not the only one.

Chapter Two

We all hold our breath as Joseph comes into view, a dog tagging along behind him. But this is no Baxter. It trails its tail between its legs, grey eyes bleak with age, grey fur covering a slim body. It is a Greyhound, but an old one. I look at the creature cautiously, pondering over my options. The safety of my Tribe has to be taken into consideration, but also the chance to meet someone new, and possibly add a member to the Tribe. Possibly. Either way, this dog doesn't look the type to be locked away, so I reckon we'll be seeing it around a lot.

Instinctively, I move towards Sophia, and I see Ruby going to protect Sapphire, who is still taking in this new arrival. Joseph smiles, unclipping the dog from a worn lead, picking up Sophia and I, then sitting down and placing us both in his lap.

I curl up, Sophia nestles into me, and I take another good look at the dog. It's a female, and seems to be tired, as it is lying down at the foot of the Armchair. Joseph doesn't seem to mind, so I relax; maybe this new arrival isn't such a bad thing after all.

Hours pass, and the dog stays still, while Joseph slowly but surely drifts off to sleep. As soon as he is asleep, Ruby leaps lightly to the floor, landing perfectly, then walking up to the Greyhound and meowing.

"Wake up, dog." She says, patting its head gently with her foot. It stirs, and gets to its feet slowly.

"Why, hello!" It smiles, a smile unlike anything we have seen a dog do before. "I'm Tess."

"Ruby." Ruby replies.

"I suppose we'll be sharing this house?" Tess enquires.

"Well, Joseph seems to want that, so yes." Ruby looks to me, and I stand up, trying not to disturb a sleeping Sophia, drop to the floor and look Tess in the eye.

"Tell me, Tess," I start, "Are all dogs out there like you?"

"Like me?" She sounds confused, so I try to explain my question.

"So... nice. You see, we already have a dog here..."

"If you can even call it a dog." Ruby interrupts me. "More like a slavering beast!"

"Ah, so that is the 'old dog' he was talking about." Tess smiles. "No, most dogs are not like me. They are bouncy, excitable creatures with untameable courage and energy. But a select few are quieter, more reserved. A little like me."

I decide that I like Tess, there and then. A cat goes by its instincts, common sense and general knowledge, and all three of those things tell me that Tess is a good companion to have, not to mention that she is going to live in our house anyway, if we like it or not, so we might as well get used to her.

"Tess, would you like to join our Tribe?" I ask, a little uncertain of her answer.

"A Tribe? But aren't they just for cats?"

"Well, usually. But our Tribe is already pretty unusual, and you seem to be the most cat-like dog - in a good way - that we've ever seen."

"Certainly!"

I breath a sigh of relief. If she had chose to not be in the Tribe, then Sapphire wouldn't trust her. Sapphire doesn't trust anyone who is not in the Tribe, except Joseph of course. Tess continues to talk with me and Ruby for a little while, before casually asking about Sophia's parents.

"We don't know." I reply, checking that Sophia is still asleep, then turning back to Tess. "She came here a few months after the twins, and I have protected her since then."

"Poor girl." Tess sighs. I agree. It's a horrible thing, not knowing who your parents are. I should know. "Well, at least she's got you."

"At least." I nod, before returning to my position in Joseph's lap.

After that, the night goes on, with everyone falling asleep rather quickly. I briefly wonder why Tess is here. Old dogs usually have families, or at least owners, to take care of them, but this is obviously not the case with Tess.

The morning comes slowly, but I soon find myself awake, the cold fingers of dawn stretching through a stained window and waking most of us up. But something's wrong. As I look around, I am no longer in Joseph's lap. He is nowhere to be found! Where on earth has he gone? I meow worriedly to Ruby, who is still half asleep.

"Where is Joseph?"

"Huh?" She yawns, stretches, then freezes, finally figuring out what is wrong. "I don't know... the Kitchen?"

"Let's check."

But somehow, I don't think he's going to be in the Kitchen. And I'm right. There's not a trace of him anywhere, not even the faintest scent.

"Maybe he just went out?" Tess offers, having just been woken up by Ruby.

"He never goes out this early." The anxiety must have shown in my voice, as Tess comes closer and nuzzles me gently.

"It's going to be just fine. You have a Tribe to sort out. I've got a crazy dog to befriend."

"Baxter!" I exclaim. "What?!?"

"He might know where Joseph went." She shrugs, before wandering into the kitchen.

Sophia has woken up, and I immediately go to comfort her. She asks, in her ever so meek voice, where Joseph has gone, and all I can say to her is that he's going to be back soon. But I'm not sure I really believe that myself. Sophia seems nervous, so I curl up on the Armchair with her. It seems so empty without Joseph, but I'm sure he's just gone out to get cat-food, or even dog-food.

Speaking of dogs, growling and barking from the kitchen tells me that Tess is trying to speak to Baxter. Her calm tones are the complete opposite of Baxter's harsh barks, so I decide to stay with Sophia and the Twins until Baxter has calmed down. But, despite still feeling a need to stay away, after ten long minutes I peer carefully into the kitchen, and marvel at the sight.

A dog is sitting there, facing Tess. Calm, skinny, and certainly not frenzied, this dog is fully white, except for a small brown spot over his right eye. The spitting image of Baxter, just behaving in a way unlike any I've ever seen Baxter behave in. Tess is talking to him, using slow, calm words that seem to have an almost magical effect on him.

"Now, Baxter," She says, her grey eyes locked onto the dog's brown ones, "Remember what you have to do."

"Apologise." Baxter's voice is nothing like I thought it would be. It sounds light-hearted, and even slightly ashamed.

"That's right." Tess keeps using a sort of motherly tone with him, before standing up and nodding her head in the direction of the Living-Room. "They're through there."

I walk back to the Armchair, still amazed at what I have seen. Ruby is talking to Sophia, Sapphire listening intently, and, from what I can hear, it seems to be words of reassurance. Good old Ruby. She looks up as I come closer, smiling as I jump up to my spot at the top of the Armchair. But something catches her attention, and her jaw drops. Sophia turns to see what she's looking at, gives a squeak of fright and hides behind Ruby, Sapphire doing the same. When I look, I see why.

Tess is walking in, Baxter behind her. When he sees us cats, he smiles, before trying to hide behind Tess, which fails disastrously, as Tess is at least three times thinner than he is. Finally, he just walks beside her. Ruby hisses, and moves to protect Sapphire and Sophia. I leap down from the Armchair and approach Baxter, with a little caution.

"So, you are the infamous Baxter." I start. "Nice to meet you, at last."

"Same here." He replies. "Just wanted to say to you all, about all that scary stuff I did back, you know, since about ten minutes ago, I'm sorry."

I nod, looking back at Ruby. She still doesn't trust Baxter, but comes up behind me and nods her head at the dog.

"Ruby. Nice to meet you. Try anything, and you're dead." She says the last part so harshly that I'm sure she means it, but Baxter doesn't seem to mind.

"Nice to meet you too." He looks back at Sophia and Sapphire. "Who're they?"

"Sophia and Sapphire." I reply, before Ruby can say anything. "Sophia's the kitten. Now, can you tell us anything about where Joseph went?"

"Joseph? Oh, the guy who owns this place." He says, and I nod. "Sorry, no. I heard him leave though. Went out at about the middle of the night. I only know that because he usually feeds me then, but he didn't. Because he went out."

"Ok. Well, he's still gone, so.. make yourself at home, I suppose? It is your house too."

"Thanks!"

He sniffs around the room, scratching and digging at some rubbish, before finding himself a suitable place to rest and lying down. Slight hunger gnaws at my stomach, but I ignore it, and go back to my place at the top of the Armchair.

Tess lies down at the foot of the Armchair, covered by the worn blanket that I am sure I gave to Sophia but must have fell onto the floor, and the Twins resume their normal positions, Sophia looking very alone and lying on the seat of the Armchair.

Sighing, I decide that it's probably time for a cat nap, so I curl up and close my eyes, all worrying thoughts disappearing quickly, and sleep soon taking over.

Chapter Three

"I want to know where I sleep!"

"You'll have to ask Shadow, Baxter."

"But he's still asleep!"

The strains of a conversation fill my ears, as I slowly blink and stretch out. Judging by the light from the window, I would say it is late afternoon, and Sophia is still asleep. Ruby is batting at a fly with her front paws, Sapphire watching, and Tess is talking to Baxter. Once he sees I'm awake, Baxter comes flying over.

"Shadow, where do I sleep?" He asks. "You all sleep on the Armchair, and Tess sleeps on the floor next to the Armchair, but that means I don't have anywhere to sleep!"

"Make a den. We cats have." I yawn, glancing around the room. No Joseph. "Use the rubbish and whatever's lying around."

"Cool!"

This seems to be an amazing idea to him, as he speeds around, digging here and there, scraping and scratching at the rubbish and dragging things everywhere. Sophia wakes up, and I go to talk to her. She wants to know if Joseph's back, but I am forced to say no, and the look on her face breaks my heart.

Quickly, I add that he could be back any

minute now, or maybe in a couple of hours. She then looks at Baxter, and I can guess what she's thinking: that dog is a lunatic. Or something along those lines. He gets so excited about the tiniest of things, the complete opposite of what a cat does; we control our emotions and only show other people what we want them to see.

Dogs, on the other hand, do as they please, and don't care who sees them or what those people think about them. Baxter has finished his 'den', which seems to be a hole in the rubbish, lined with a few blankets and ripped clothes (How did he find those? I have no idea). Nothing like our homes, but hey; he is a dog. Tess is going over to talk to him, while Ruby continues swatting at the fly, Sapphire's attention drawn to something on the far side of the room... but it isn't a rat. It's a pipe, strangely enough, with a leak in it. A leak that is dripping water. Water! Just what we need!

"Baxter!" I call. He looks at me and cocks his head. "Please come to the kitchen."

"Ok!"

Once in the kitchen, I start attempting to open cupboards. Luckily, most of them have gaps in or under the doors, so they are very easy to get a grip on. As soon as they are open, I scour the cupboards for a small pan. Unfortunately, Joseph never really did much cooking, but I manage to find a small plastic box that will do just fine, in the depths of one of the larger cupboards.

"Baxter, please grab this for me and bring it through to the living-room."

"Uh, ok.."

I can tell that he's not quite sure what I'm doing, but I know it will work, and he trusts me, so he follows me into the living-room, box in mouth. Everyone is looking at me now, all wondering what on earth I am doing, except Sapphire, who gives me a knowing look and the smallest of smiles. I nod back, guiding Baxter to the pipe and positioning the box in such a way that the water drips into it. The dog suddenly realises what I am doing, and is quick to try and tell everyone else, but they've already figured it out and simply ignore him.

As soon as I have nothing to do, however, hunger slips into my mind, and once it is there I just can't get it out. I look around, and everyone else seems to be having the same thought. Baxter starts digging in the rubbish again, this time bringing out half a bag of old cat biscuits. Ruby is quick to take them off him, as his violent shaking of the bag is making most of the biscuits fly out, and we start to eat. But I feel sorry for the dogs. Especially Tess. After a little bit of thought, I push one of the biscuits over to her.

"Try it." I offer.

"Are you sure?" She asks, hesitant.

"Better than starving." I reply, and, after a second of deliberation, she nods, tentatively nibbling on the fish shaped biscuit. At first, she makes a slight face of disgust, but bites at it again, and again. I smile; Tess really is the most cat-like dog I've ever met.

"Thanks!" She smiles, settling down at the foot of the Armchair and closing her eyes.

"Can I try one?" Baxter asks. I shrug, and bat one over to him, the big dog ripping at it violently and biting with his powerful jaws, and getting a mouthful of rubbish!

Spitting and coughing, Baxter's face turns to one of utter disgust, and we all laugh. Shaking his head, he tells us all he's 'never trying one again', before grabbing another one, more carefully, and eating it slowly. Ruby cuts one up with her claws for Sophia to eat, and Tess continues to eat carefully. I eat one myself, and the taste is musty but satisfying.

Suddenly, Baxter's eyes widen, and he turns around, looking at the area he destroyed in search of the cat biscuits. He whines, pawing at the ground, and I have no idea what he's doing. Neither does anyone else, until he looks at us and cries:

"My den! I destroyed my den!"

It is then that I realise he has dug straight through the hole he made and called a den. Shaking my head, I decide to make him happy.

"I'll make you a den. A proper one." I say, and his eyes light up. "But you have to help."

"Sure!"

"I'll help too." Tess says, and soon Ruby says she'll help too, as soon as she's finished her cat biscuits.

I get to work straight away, as Tess tries to calm down an ecstatic Baxter, finding a dry spot by the window, where an old radiator spurts out tiny bits of warmth every few minutes. Baxter digs out all the rubbish, revealing a deep red carpet. I didn't even know we had a carpet! I then sort through all the rubbish that Baxter's unearthed, and find some sort of broken suitcase. It doesn't take the large dog long to rip it apart, and push it into the hole he's made. From there, finding soft-looking things with the help of Ruby and lining the half-suitcase with them, Tess helping as well, is easy, and soon Baxter has a half decent den.

"Don't destroy this one," I warn him, "Or I won't make you another one."

"I'll be careful!" He assures me, before lying down in his new den.

I then go back to the Armchair, where Sapphire is staring out the window. Well, I say out, but you can't really see much, just muddled colours and light, so it's more like she's just staring at the window. Sophia is curled up next to Ruby, who nods at me before moving over to where Sapphire is, and I take her place by Sophia. The beautiful young kitten nestles her tiny body into mine, and is soon fast asleep. For a while, I keep looking at the door anxiously: when will Joseph be back? It's getting scary, the fact that he's not been here for almost an entire day, if what Baxter said about him going out around midnight is right. The threatening thought that he might never come back lingers at the back of my mind, but I don't want to acknowledge it. Joseph will come back, he has to. He loved us, like his own children. He wouldn't just leave... would he?

"When do you reckon he'll be back?" Ruby asks, as she and Sapphire lie down properly, and Sapphire curls up into Ruby.

"Soon." I reply softly. "It has to be soon."

She nods, but a look of uncertainty crosses her face, and I understand, since that's how I feel too. He has to be back any time now. But, as I look around, the emptiness seems to close in, and I worry about what we'll do if Joseph really is gone forever. We can't survive off rats and rubbish, and there's no way even our claws can get those cans of cat-food open.

But I have to stay strong. For my Tribe, and for Sophia. She is so young, to have all of this thrown at her, so I'll have to guard her from the horrors of our situation. That is, if Joseph doesn't come back. He could come strolling in the door any minute now, but something in my mind doubts it. And something else, something I haven't really felt before, tells me I don't want him to come back, because there would be a reason why he left, and it could be a bad one. What if he's not interested in us anymore, and comes back just to throw us out? But that's impossible, he adored, no, still adores us, and we adore him back. It's impossible that he could not love us anymore.

Yet something still nags me from the back of my mind, in those deep depths that I don't like to explore. Either Joseph doesn't want to come back, or something's keeping him away, and I don't want to know which it is.

Chapter Four

The night comes quickly, darkness covering everywhere, but there is still no sign of Joseph. With a heavy heart, I tell everyone that they should go to their dens, since it is very cold this particular night. They agree, but with an air of sadness which is almost unbearable to witness.

I jump into my cardboard box, Sophia following me. She always sleeps in my den on the cooler nights, when we simply cannot sleep on the Armchair with no shelter from the freezing wind that seems to blow in everywhere. She snuggles into the warmth of my body and the many blankets I have in my den, looking up at me with sleepy eyes.

"Will... Joseph... be back... soon?" She murmurs, on the brink of sleep.

"Yes, Sophia. Probably tomorrow."

She nods, although I think she is too sleepy to understand what I am saying, and, about a second later, is fast asleep. I pull a blanket over us with my teeth, the exhausting events of the day all piling up into one word: sleep. I need sleep. And it comes, too, but it brings with it dreams, dreams of memories that I would rather forget.

I am wandering down a street. It is in a town, and the rain is pouring down, cars racing by and soaking anyone walking past with water from puddles on the road. One of these cars hits me with some water, and I hiss. It is true that cats do not like water; in fact, most loathe it. I am one of those.

The people walking down the street take no notice of me, their umbrellas up and minds set on getting home. It is late afternoon, but no sunlight can be seen, only drab greys and blacks in the sky.

At this moment in time, I am young, and, you could say, free. Free from a family who love you and feed you, and a house that offers warmth, protection and shelter. Being free is not necessarily a good thing. My paws hurt from walking so long, and I'm shivering from the cold that is everywhere. Whenever I stop, people shoo me on, like I am some sort of stray. Well, I suppose I am, but there's no need to shout about it.

Inside, I am respectable and pleasant, loyal and obedient, but nobody sees that side of me. They all see the rough street cat with a bad temper that's been out in the rain too long. They see the tough show that I put on to survive, and think it's the real me. It isn't. But how am I supposed to tell them that?

I finally reach a back alley, which seems empty. At last, a chance to rest! Slowly, I slide myself underneath a large bin with wheels, finally safe from the pelting rain. But I still don't sleep. I am always alert, ready to defend this alleyway like it is a castle. But the time never comes, and, finally, I start to sleep. The thudding of rain on the bin and the footsteps of people on the pavement are what I focus on, listen to, and they help. Soon, I fall into deep sleep, and everything goes black.

"Shadow..."

I wake up suddenly. That... was a bad dream. More like a bad memory, actually. Sophia is still in my den with me, but she is very much awake, and has a look on her face that I know full well to be hunger.

"I know, Sophia." I yawn, stretching but staying in a lying position. "We'll figure something out. Now, how's about we wake the others up?"

She nods, and hops out of the box. I follow quickly, and go straight to the Twins' Fortress. They are curled up inside, and you can't tell which is which, since they are sharing a single blanket and lying on the same pillow. Or is it just a bundle of old clothes? Either way, I pad softly over and brush one of their faces gently with my tail.

"Ruby... Sapphire... time to get up..." I say, in a low enough pitch as to not startle them, but so that they can still hear me.

Amazingly, the one that I haven't touched wakes up first, and I can tell that it's Sapphire, since expert mousers need the absolute best hearing and sight. She pats Ruby lightly with her paw, before standing back as Ruby springs up and spins around, sees she is in no danger, then turns to me.

"Morning Ruby, Sapphire." I nod.

"Nice day to eat, don't you think?" Ruby asks.

"Not really a nice day." I flick my tail towards a window, where rain is thudding, albeit gently, on the glass.

"Still. I am hungry, and so's Sapphire."

"If I had food to give to you..." I start, but Ruby cuts me off.

"Don't worry, we'll find something. Come on Sapphire; there's bound to be some rats or mice in here somewhere."

The Twins walk off, heading into the Living-Room, while I go to wake up the dogs, Sophia following me closely. Tess is already half up, eyes open but still lying in bed, so I give her a nod and a quiet 'Morning' before I try to wake up a sleeping Baxter. And that is a hard task. He snores, grunts, rolls over, barks, and all before he finally wakes up. Nothing like a cat, that's for sure!

As soon as he is fully awake, I tell him that Sapphire and Ruby are hunting for rats and mice, but he can always sniff around for some food. Baxter takes this opportunity at once, racing around and sniffing here and there, but he has enough sense to give Sapphire and Ruby their space.

I then wander over in the Twins' direction. Sapphire has froze, staring at a hole in the wall, and Ruby is by her side, eyes fixed on the same spot. After about ten seconds, a rat sneaks out, quite large in size and black in colour. It has its back to us, so Sapphire crouches and prepares to spring, eyes locked on her target. Time seems to freeze as she leaps forwards, silently, like an assassin, and pounces on the rat, silencing its squeaks with a single bite.

"Well done." I meow to her, and she turns, rat in mouth, a smile on her face. She then cocks her head, as if to ask if I want some. I refuse politely, saying I'm going to find my own food, smiling slightly when Sapphire cuts Sophia a piece of the rat.

But I don't look for rats. I have my own place for mousing, a small corner in the kitchen, which the little creatures just seem to love. I like to be alone as much as possible, to gather my thoughts and properly think things through without interruption, so having a place where only I go is very important to me. Now, as I stay hidden under some rubbish, I reflect on everything that has happened, and also something that hasn't happened yet. Joseph has still not returned, and I fear he shall never do so.

But good things have happened as well. Baxter, the petrifying beast that we have feared for years, has turned out to be a helpful, if easily excitable, companion, as well as good entertainment in the long hours when we are wishing for our owner to come home.

And it's not even just that. Everyone has grown closer to each other, as we need to be there for each other all the time, and helping out your fellow cat (Or dog, I suppose) is more important than ever.

But I still want Joseph to come back, and I think we need him. In fact, I know we need him. We can't be house cats with no owner; it's simply not possible. Then there's the thought that someone would try and rescue us, but I don't want to think about that. Joseph will come back. He has to.

Suddenly, I see a small head poke up out of the rubbish, and smile. Dinner. It scurries up, looks around, then freezes, staring straight at me with two beady black eyes. Then I pounce. And, if you are in awe of Sapphire's skills and neat way of dispatching rats, then look away. I leap, grab the mouse in one claw, then bite. Today must be a good day, as I don't get blood absolutely everywhere, and the mouse tastes relatively nice, but that's probably just down to me being so hungry.

After grabbing another mouse, and eating it quickly, I walk over to the leaking water pipe, and the plastic box that is half full with water. I wet my paws and groom myself, before having a drink and wandering back over in the Twins' direction. Tess is fully awake and lying near them, Ruby is cutting up rats and Sapphire is lying near them, probably tired from catching... is that fifteen whole rats?! And they've probably ate a few already.

But the rats seem thin, almost as if they're running out of food. A little like us. A lot like us, actually. I wonder what we'll do if the rodent supply runs out... we can't starve, can we?

Chapter Five

It's been five days. Five sunrises, five sunsets, and Joseph is still not back. I have to admit that even I have my doubts as to if he will actually come back or not. Everyone is really thin, and hungry all the time, since the rodent population in the house has dwindled considerably in the last few days. The dogs - yes, Tess too - have been chewing on rubbish desperately, trying to find even a morsel of food, but to no avail. Us cats have been scouring the house, and the cupboards, but most food is locked away, inaccessible or we are unable to open the packaging it is in. We are starving.

I wander wearily in the direction of the kitchen, to check the cupboards once more and attempt to open the fridge, sometimes slipping on rubbish due to pure exhaustion and hunger. No one has been sleeping well, since starving makes it extremely hard to drift off at night, and Sophia has even been suffering from nightmares. Each night is as cold and uncomfortable as the last, so I keep Sophia close to me at all times.

As I get to the kitchen, I see Baxter running around in some sort of craze, jumping at a shelf as if he were trying to knock whatever was on it onto the floor! I quickly move to stop him, but it's too late, and a load of tins come tumbling to the floor. Tins... cat-food! Some tins even burst open as they hit the floor (Well, the junk that covers the floor) and the smell is amazing! I look up at Baxter in surprise.

"You... are... a genius!" I smile, turning around and meowing loudly. "Food!"

"Food?" Tess answers my call first, loping over to Baxter and giving him a motherly smile, before licking up some cat-food.

"What are you talking abo... food!" Ruby yells, racing over to a can with Sapphire close behind her.

Sophia comes in soon after, a small smile lighting up her face as she scrambles to some food, starting to eat straight away. I do the same, and it tastes amazing! I suppose it would do, as we've been starving for the last five days, but still. I watch Sophia carefully, to make sure she doesn't cut herself on the sharp edge of the tin, and take a second look at the shelf. It is no wonder that we didn't already find those cans; you can hardly see them from a cat's height. But dogs are taller, so it is only natural that Baxter, who is much larger than all us cats, saw the cans first. He's not too bad... for a dog anyway.

"Who found them?" Ruby asks, a little later on, as we all gather around the Armchair, Baxter lying by Tess' side.

"Baxter did." I reply, smiling again at the excitable dog.

"I'm proud of you." Tess says to Baxter, who just grins.

"It's what family's for, right?"

I think over his words for a few minutes, repeating them over in my head. 'It's what family's for'. Baxter thinks of the Tribe as his family, and I am glad to say that the feeling is mutual. He has lived with us for so long, been a feared enemy that was never to be faced, but in a matter of days our perspective on him has changed entirely. An opinion that we built up after years and years, just gone in an instant. Well, not exactly an instant, more like a very short period of time. But, as I look at all the animals I think of as family in this room, I couldn't be happier. Unless Joseph was here.

Our old owner has been on my mind a lot. Reasons and theories flit around in my head like little flies, but I don't like paying attention to any of them. They all end badly,

36

and I really don't need all those negative thoughts on my mind at the moment. No one does. Negative thoughts make for a negative attitude, especially if you bottle them all up. I have known many a cat (And dog) suddenly explode and take out everything on whoever is nearest to them, and it is not nice at all. I can tell you that because I have experienced this myself, first hand, on both sides of the scenario.

As the sun sets, and darkness crawls slowly across everything, I decide that we should all head to bed, and we cats bid the dogs goodnight. Sophia follows me to my cardboard box den like usual, and we curl up inside together, her white fur mixing with my black fur. She gets to sleep fairly quickly, but I stay awake, hearing sounds every so often that make me jump and make my heart race, but our front door never opens, and Joesph never comes. After a few hours of this, I am prepared to sleep, but Sophia whines suddenly, tossing and turning, batting her little paws at something I cannot see. Another nightmare.

Sighing, I nestle my body into hers, putting my paws around her, and she eventually relaxes. I am finally able to close my eyes, and sleep soundly, knowing that Sophia is ok. The rays of sunlight that slowly creep into the house are what wake me in the early morning, however, spreading their warmth around the house. Sophia is still asleep, so I relax into the comfort of my bedding and take some time to think over everything that has happened.

The most prominent thought in my mind, at the moment, is Baxter, and everything he has done for us. And himself, actually. I am determined to thank him in some way other than speech, and I've got an idea that might just work.

Wriggling my way out of den but not disturbing Sophia is a hard task, but also one that only takes me around five minutes, as I quickly get out and move over to the cupboards in the kitchen. From there, I carefully open them one by one, searching for something. It isn't in the lower cupboards, so I jump up onto the counter top and look all over there, then cast my eyes onto the shelves that surround the kitchen. I see what I need, but it is quite far away, and high up, however I think of the perfect solution.

The Twins' den is just below the shelf

that I need to get to, so I jump off the counter top, scramble over to the Twins' den, then take a deep breath. This is going to work. This has to work. I step onto the first level of tins, then the next, and the next, until I'm at the top. The shelf isn't too far away, so I jump up and catch the top of it with my two front paws, pulling myself up, then going over to a large tin labelled: 'Chunky Dog-Food'. Perfect. Baxter shouldn't have to eat cat-food, especially when he's done so much to help us. It's just my way of paying him back, in a good way.

 I look down from the shelf. The Twins' den would be in danger if I were to try and bat the tin down in that direction, but the other end of the shelf leads down to a relatively clear area. If I just bat it like this, with my paw, then like this... the metallic grey can is nearing the edge of the shelf, so I take care with how I push it, making sure that it doesn't fall onto something important. A final prod from my paw makes it fall to the ground with a loud 'Clang!', and I quickly get down from the shelf. Everyone rushes into the kitchen, and as soon as Baxter sniffs the air, he quivers in excitement.

 "Shadow!" He exclaims, bounding over

to me. "Look at this!"

"Looks to me like someone wanted to thank you for what you did." Tess gives me a knowing smile, and I shrug, smiling back.

"Cool!" He runs over to it, eating quickly, but Tess stands back. I cock my head in her direction.

"You not having any?" I ask.

"He deserves it, for all he's done. He's clever, that pup, if a little over enthusiastic at times."

"You can say that again." I mutter, and she just chuckles.

"Give him a chance. You'll be surprised." She promises, before going into the Living Room.

Baxter is happy for the rest of the day, and it seems to rub off on everyone else. Ruby stops snapping at everyone, which is her reaction to being really tired, and Sapphire doesn't mind being around Tess and Baxter too much. Tess also makes her sleeping place a little better, digging into it a little bit and covering some parts with soft materials like small blankets and torn old clothes.

But when the day is drawing to a close and darkness has almost arrived, Tess has an idea for the evening. Usually, we are just hunting for food and things to keep us warm, but today is different. She says that, as Baxter has done something special, she feels that it is her turn to show, or rather tell, us something very personal and important to her. It is something that even I am yet to share with the Tribe, as I feel that it makes up who you are, and should only be shared with people you truly know and trust, and only when you are ready to tell them. It is the story of her past.

Chapter Six

"I was born," Tess starts, in her slow and patient voice, "A great many years ago, too many for me to remember now. As a young Greyhound, my coat was sleek and black, my eyes bold and a beautiful bright blue. My future was determined, not by me, but my owner; I was trained from a very young age to be in the races.

'Now, you cats may not have heard of the Greyhound races, so I will tell you a little about them. Greyhounds are lined up in cage-like structures, and are released when the race begins. A mechanical rabbit, which we have been trained to chase, speeds around the track in front of us, urging us to go faster. The winner is whoever gets back to where you started first, as the track is a never ending oval, after a certain amount of laps. The result of the race is betted on by men, and sometimes women, who like to watch the sport.

'As it was - and still is - a very competitive business, only the very best dogs were kept, and my owner believed that I was one of the very best. 'Shadowy Champion' was my race name, and I believe that many men and women betted on me to win. And I did win, lots of times, against many different dogs. But my owner soon lost his affection for me, kicking me if I even dared to come in 2nd, and God save me if I ever came below that.

'But as long as I kept winning, I kept on my owner's good side. However, that was not to last." A long sigh escapes Tess' muzzle, as she puts her head down onto her paws, and Baxter lies closer to her, his head resting on her back.

"Whatever happened?" Ruby asks.

"What happened?" Tess gives Ruby a small, sad smile. "What happens to everyone after a good few years? They grow older, they win less, and they become too tired to train. Their owners lose patience and think that they're 'a waste of space' or 'not putting enough effort in', then they kick them out onto the streets and focus their attention on newer, younger and faster dogs."

"He just kicked you onto the street?!" Baxter exclaims, growling a little.

"Baxter, what is done is done, and cannot be changed." Tess calms the younger dog down, and I marvel at the way she handles him so well. "Anyway, it is not like I wished to keep racing. It is a cruel sport, and, as I matured, I learned that it was not the right way to live. But neither is living on the streets, wandering from place to place. No one wants an old dog on their last legs, but the other strays love to torment the old, weak and helpless. It is their entertainment, I believe, although I am not quite sure. It may just be instincts."

"How dare they?! I'm going to kill 'em, ma!" Baxter barks, before realising what he has added on the end and quickly stuttering an apology.

"It's fine, Baxter. I'll be your ma if you want me to be, but I think you'll need some help if you want to go around killing every single stray on the streets!" Tess chuckles, and Baxter curls up closer to her. "But I reckon now is time to sleep, for everyone. It's been a long night."

I yawn, as we all say our 'good nights', and I look back at Baxter and, more importantly, Tess. She really is like the mother figure in his life, and he loves her back, I just know it. It's good that Baxter has some sense of stability in his life now, in the form of Tess. She is the one who calms him down, and always sees the best in everyone. She sees the good in all of us, even though it may not be visible to others. A true hero, is our old Tess.

Sophia pads after me like usual, as we scramble up the mountain of rubbish that leads to the kitchen, then climb into the cardboard box. But before she goes to sleep, she looks up at me with tired eyes.

"Shadow.." She murmurs.

"Yes?"

"What's... my story?"

"Your story?"

I sigh. A young kitten like Sophia shouldn't have such a tragic past, but she does, so I'm not telling her everything. Just a few things. The bare necessities, you might say.

"Joseph found you in a animal shelter, in a litter of six. He took a liking to you and brought you home. Time passed, and we grew closer to you. Me, Ruby and Sapphire. We still protect you to this day."

"But... my ma?" She asks, very quietly.

"I don't know Sophia. Now, get some sleep. Don't let your past trouble you. It's the present that matters."

She nods, twisting and turning until she is comfortable, then going to sleep. But I'm not happy with myself. I should've told her the entire truth, about her ma and how she came to be in the animal shelter, but I just can't.

You see, I did know Sophia's mother. She was a lovely cat, always happy and kind to everyone, and she ignored the 'violent stray cat' stereotype completely. I even travelled with her, for a little while, and I learnt that her name was Snowdrop. She was a beautiful white colour, with long whiskers and two blue eyes that shone like gems.

But one day, when I was not with her, some older strays took advantage of her in a tight alley corner, and I only got there in time to see the cowards flee after a dog started barking somewhere close by. Snowdrop was in a bad way, but her wounds soon healed, and she found out that she was having kittens. However, a great illness had overcome her body, and I was the one who suggested to find the Animal Shelter. At first, she refused, but common sense made her change her mind.

A good amount of time later, the kittens were born, but Snowdrop was dying from the illness. Exhaustion and starvation weren't helping either. So I made a promise to her that I still haven't forgotten. I promised to always look after the kittens as best I could.

So, when she sadly passed away, I took the kittens, one by one, to the door of the Animal Shelter, and waited nearby until someone found them. It was then that I slipped away, found Snowdrop's body, and left her to rest by a rose bush in a park.

You can imagine, then, how amazed and relieved I was when Joseph came in with Sophia in one hand and a six-pack of cat-food cans in the other. Sophia was the only pure white kitten in the litter, the others taking on the dull greys and blacks of the strays, so I remembered her clearly. And when Ruby told me that Sapphire heard Joseph mumble 'Kitten ... called ... Sophia ...' I just smiled. That was just perfect. Absolutely perfect.

And, I think to myself, as I watch Sophia sleep for a while, she would be proud. Of me? Maybe. But of Sophia? Definitely. I would give anything for Snowdrop to be here now, since, out of all the strays I have ever met, she was the only one to change me. She changed me from a young, violent stray into a mature, caring adult, and I wouldn't even be in this house if it weren't for her. I know for certain that no one in their right mind picks a hissing, spitting, bundle of fury for the family pet, which is what I was once... a long, long time ago.

But I shouldn't linger on the past. What is done is done, as Tess said before, and there's nothing you can do about it. The present is enough to worry about, but if you add in the past and future it's enough to make anyone go insane! A small smile lights up my face, as I decide to sleep, darkness already covering everything, and silence blanketing the room. For once, I am going to sleep with a full stomach and an easy mind. And it feels better than anything I have ever experienced before. Dreamless sleep takes over my weary body, and peace ensues.

But, like most things in life, it is interrupted by something much more chaotic a while later. Loud crashing and banging makes me jolt awake, as my eyes dart to Sophia, and I sigh in relief as I see she's alright. But the relief is not to last. More crashing and banging makes me jump right out of the box, as I look around for the cause of the problem. It's not in the kitchen, but a very disgruntled Ruby and a frightened Sapphire are, as Ruby stalks up to me, furious.

"What on earth is happening?" She

snaps, as yet another crash is heard.

"I don't know. It sounds like it's coming from the hall though..."

"Let's go then! I swear, if this is Baxter..." She trails off, marching through the Living Room and into the hall, Sapphire following her.

I quickly chase after them both, Sophia close behind, and I see Baxter lying by Tess, looking thoroughly terrified. If it's not him that's causing the ruckus, then what is it...?

Chapter Seven

"It's stopped!"

I look up at Ruby, who is peering at something in the hall. I quickly move to see what she is so interested in, then freeze. The stairs have been unblocked. Memories flood into my head, as I follow Ruby and a hesitant Sapphire up stair after stair, dust still flying through the air. Whining from below us tells me that Baxter doesn't want to come up, but that's fine. I'm more focused on what is to come.

And I have a right to be. The upstairs is nothing like what we imagined it would look like. It is clean and neat, but everything is caked in layer upon layer of dust. My attention is quickly drawn to a door across the landing, which I push open carefully. Ruby gasps behind me, as my eyes widen.

It's a bedroom. The double bed lies there, untouched, sheets still made, duvet greyed with time, a dresser by the side of it. And on the dresser? Pictures. Pictures of the past, all in golden-looking frames.

"Shadow?" Ruby asks, quietly.

"Yes?" My voice is barely louder than a whisper.

"You never told us your story."

I don't reply, looking back at the

pictures instead. The first one is of Joseph, as a younger man, with his wife. They are both happy, smiling people, without a care in the world. I sigh. Those days are long gone.

"Joseph..." I start slowly, gazing at the first picture. "Wasn't always like he is now. He used to be young. And he used to have a wife. A beautiful young women. They were very happy together, and didn't have a care in the world."

The second picture is of Joseph and his wife again, but this time they are holding a young, black cat, Annabelle stroking its head. Even the cat seems to be smiling, two gleaming green eyes staring straight at the camera.

"I, also, used to be young." I let out a sad sigh. "But it was a long time ago. Before Joseph adopted me, I was a violent young stray, but I met a cat that showed me different ways. Nicer ways, I suppose you could say. So I kept these ideals, and got brought into an animal shelter. Then adopted by a young couple, who I know now as Joseph and Annabelle."

"But..." Baxter has walked in, staying at Tess' side. "Annabelle isn't... here... is she?"

"No." I cast my eyes to the third picture. A lonely man, now in his mid-forties, stands with his head down, dressed fully in black, an older black cat by his side, green eyes dulled and bleak. There is no happiness to be seen in this picture. "She died. Quite young. I still do not know the cause."

"This was around the time we came, wasn't it?" Ruby asks, and I nod.

"Three months later, two new cats arrived in the house. Twins. One was quiet and cautious, the other protective and loud. I didn't know that they would turn out to be two of the nicest cats I ever knew."

Two purrs, one much meeker than the other, fill the room, as Ruby and Sapphire come closer to me, rubbing against my sides. I smile. There's no two cats in the world just like Ruby and Sapphire. I then hear very small footsteps, and know that Sophia has just came into the room, as I look at the final picture. This one is of just one kitten, snow white in colour, with two bright blue eyes, and a frightened face. She looks straight at the camera, afraid and uncertain of what is to come.

"Then, a year later, a small bundle of white fur is brought into the house, probably scared out of its mind. So I make a promise, there and then, to protect her always. I soon learned that her name was Sophia. And I have protected her ever since."

That small bundle of fur skips across the dusty floor and attaches itself to my leg, as I look down, a smile on my face.

"And that is my story."

"Ok, now who's up for dinner?" Baxter barks excitedly, and we all sigh, laughing a little bit.

"Come on then, you big softie." Tess smiles, going down the stairs first, Baxter following her into the Kitchen.

The Twins then leave, Ruby slightly in front of Sapphire, and I am left alone in the room with Sophia. I expect her to go down after the others, but she wanders over to the dresser, looking up at the pictures.

"Shadow..."

"Yes?"

"Is... Joseph... really... going to... come back?" She whispers.

"Maybe, but I don't know when."

"Soon?" She offers, little blue eyes full of hope.

"Soon." I nod, hoping that he actually will come back soon. I'm having serious doubts as to whether Joseph actually will come back, after all this time. And if he doesn't... what then?

Sophia looks into my eyes for a few more seconds, before looking back at the pictures on the dresser. I move towards the stairs, then stop, looking back at her.

"Coming?"

Sophia turns around quickly and scampers towards me, and we both go down the stairs. Baxter has picked up a cat-food can with his teeth, and is repeatedly throwing it against the wall, Tess watching to make sure he doesn't hurt himself, and the Twins are sitting near a hole in the wall, waiting for rats or mice that they can catch and eat. I go over to the Armchair, climbing to my place at the top, as Sophia curls up on the seat of the Armchair. The banging of a tin against the wall is the only noise that I can hear, then the 'clang!' as the top flies off, and lands on a pile of junk.

"Finally!" Baxter laughs, picking up the can and taking it through to the Kitchen, pouring it into our bowls as well as he can. "Now for our dinner, ma!"

"Seriously?" Ruby comes up behind him, dropping the rat that she is carrying and looking at Baxter as if he is a lunatic. "You're going to go through all that again? For one can of cat-food?"

"Uh... yes?"

"Just take the rat. Sapphire's got two others and a mouse in the Living Room. Help yourselves."

"Thanks!"

Baxter bounds off in the direction of the Living-Room, Tess picking up the rat that Ruby dropped and thanking her again, before following the extremely excited Baxter into the Living-Room. Ruby goes after them, presumably to fetch Sapphire, while me and Sophia tuck into the cat-food in our bowls. It has a slightly musty taste, but, for the most part, is quite satisfying. Eating from a food bowl makes me think of Joseph, and how he always used to feed us. Sadness clouds my mind, so, once I've finished eating, I leap up to the window sill and look out of the smudged and dirtied glass.

I can't actually see through the window, but I can see the light that comes through. It is different colours, green in places, whitish-yellow in others, and a faint brown is somewhere, but nothing apart from that. Most of the windows in the house are like this, some even smashed and bordered up, like the one in what used to be Baxter's room. The windows upstairs are too dust and cobweb covered for even the faintest light to get through, which is why the upstairs is in never-ending darkness.

Time passes, minutes turn to hours, but I stay put, my thoughts and memories taking me back to times I would rather forget, but also the better times. Memories of Sophia, Snowdrop, even meeting Joseph for the first time. That was certainly a time to remember.

I am locked in a small cage, and many other cats are locked up in cages to my left and right, and even above and below me. But I do not yowl, or stalk to the back of the cage and sulk. I, instead, curl up and face the strange people who are in the room, and wonder why anyone would ever pick up a cat that was hissing and spitting at them, like the strange person that is trying to pick up a ginger tom, who certainly does not want to be touched.

But when the bars of my cage rattle open, I am surprised. A hand comes in, and picks me up, so I go with it, remembering words of guidance from Snowdrop (May she rest in eternal peace) and purring when another hand pats my head, stroking my silky black coat. Yes, I have been washed since I came into the Animal Shelter, as before my coat was a mixture of blacks, greys and browns, and was very matted, but that just tends to happen to street cats. There isn't much time for grooming, when you are constantly defending yourself or scavenging for food.

In fact, there isn't much time for anything. You either get shooed on by humans, scared off by dogs or fought off by other cats. It's not a nice life, certainly, but I have never even considered any other way of living. Being in a house, with food brought to you everyday, would be a blessing, with owners to love and fondle you and sometimes even other cats to flounder around with. It is a life of luxury and constant satisfaction, the life of a House Cat.

And, I think to myself, as the stroking continues and a woman comes up behind the man, it is a life that I crave. I think that any cat wants a warm home with loving owners, but not many cats get to experience that dream. These people could make that dream come true for me...

"Now then, Annabelle, how's about this

beauty?" The man who has picked me up turns to a woman next to him.

"He's certainly handsome." She remarks, running her hand down my back. "And he's doesn't look like the kind to scratch or bite. I think he'll do just fine."

"But what on earth should we call him?" The man asks.

"Shadow. We'll call him Shadow. Just look at the colour of his fur!"

"Then Shadow will be his name!" The man laughs heartily, and the woman laughs along with him. I have a feeling that this is going to be work out...

Chapter Eight

"Shadow..."

"Wh...what?"

I wake up from my daze hurriedly, snapping my head round to see Ruby up on the window sill next to me.

"You were up here ages, so I came to check if you were alright." She says in a gentle voice.

"I'm fine. Just... remembering."

"I understand."

Glancing down, I see Sapphire lying near the window sill. Of course; the Twins are never far apart. When she sees me looking, Sapphire gives me the smallest of smiles, before rolling over and purring. At least, I think she's purring, but she's so quiet that I can't actually tell. Either way, Ruby, after a few seconds of silence, hops off the window sill and goes over to her twin, the two of them exchanging almost soundless conversation, until Baxter comes rushing into the room, for some unknown but probably absurd reason. As soon as he enters, they abruptly leave, Ruby even going as far as to hiss at him as they move into the Living-Room.

"Hey Shadow!" He bounds over, with bundles of unstoppable energy, like usual.

"Hello." My bored monotone does nothing to dissuade his excitement, sadly.

"Does Ruby not like me?" A slight note of sadness can be heard in his voice, as I look into his slightly doleful eyes.

"I shouldn't think so." I reply, attempting to reassure the ever changing Baxter. "She just doesn't like dogs much."

"Why not? I think we're amazing!" He barks loudly, and I have to smile at that innocent and slightly naive remark.

"Ruby and Sapphire... they've had some, let's say, unfortunate run ins with dogs, in the past." I sigh at the word 'unfortunate': it's a major understatement.

"What happened?" His curiosity is just as untameable as his excitement, sadly, so I simply shake my head and look towards the Living-Room.

"I'm not the best cat to tell you. Ask Ruby, tonight. She'll explain. And maybe you can tell everyone why dogs are so 'amazing'." I just have to add that last part, to lift the sombre mood that seems to have clouded over our brief conversation.

"Cool!" Is all Baxter says, before he too goes to the Living-Room.

I let him leave, glad of the peace and

quiet, before scanning my eyes over the Kitchen. It seems so desolate, without the shuffling Joseph around to feed us and give us water, to pet us and mumble to Sapphire. I miss him, more than I've ever missed anyone ever before, and yearn to even see his face for a few seconds, to sniff the faintest hint of his scent, but it's just like he's disappeared off the face of the earth... I sincerely hope that isn't the case.

After a few minutes of tranquility, I decide to check on the others, leaping off the window sill and padding over the mountain of junk that leads to the Living Room. Everyone is gathered, for a change, around Baxter's den, the 'half-suitcase', Tess telling Sophia some sort of fictional story about a small princess kitten in a huge castle, and she seems to like it, as she is smiling when she looks up at me.

"Good story?" Sophia grins at me.

"Very good." She whispers shyly.

"Well, I believe that good stories tend to go down better with good food, do they not?" I direct my gaze at Baxter.

"Food, cat-food, I'll get it now!" He races into the Kitchen, and I wince slightly as banging and clanging ensues.

But, after around a minute, he emerges from the Kitchen victorious, bringing three cans of cat-food into the Living-Room, placing them down in front of us, then going back into the Kitchen and bringing us our bowls. Ruby keeps her distance, Sapphire too, as they cautiously eat out of their bowls, once Baxter fills them, and Tess continues to spin Sophia fantastical tales, of faraway places and riches beyond compare, until the light from the windows grows darker, and night time is upon us.

Just before we all retire to our dens, however, Baxter surprises Ruby and Sapphire by speaking directly to them, something he usually would never dare to do.

"Ruby..." He starts, his voice wavering a little from nervousness.

"What is it?" She snaps, rather unkindly, having taken quite the disliking to the excitable dog.

"Well... I was talking to Shadow... and I asked why you don't like me..."

"You finally noticed?" The sarcasm seems to drip from her words, as she stares daggers at Baxter.

"Uh... yes... and he said you had some...

uh... unfortunate... run ins with... dogs..."

"You can say that again." She snorts, but with less sarcasm, and quickly directs a slightly confused look at me, but I just shrug and flick my tail in Baxter's direction.

"And... when I asked... he said you would be better to explain... what happened..."

"Well." She starts, but pauses, as if unsure on how to reply, for once in her life, looking at Sapphire and talking almost inaudibly with her, before turning back to the rest of us. "I suppose you should know. How we... lived. Before we were adopted by Joseph."

She turns to Sapphire once more, as we all wait patiently for them to finish their practically silent conversation. Baxter looks relieved, if a little hurt by Ruby's choice of words. I send him a reassuring look, which he returns with a grateful, but small, smile. Sophia walks over to me and lies down in between my legs, as Tess goes to lie by Baxter, in his den, and he snuggles into her, clearly grateful of the company. Finally, Ruby turns back to us, Sapphire lying by her side, but Ruby sits up, ready to tell us her - and Sapphire's - story.

"It was a long time ago, when me and

Sapphire were born. We were only two of a seven strong litter, the eldest being a bully of a kitten called Tyrone, or Ty for short. We both had different names back then, names our mother chose for us. I was Brie, and Sapphire was Whisper.

'We grew up on the streets, as alleycats, our mother guiding us through the dingy underground and always finding us food and shelter. But, when we were old enough, we would venture out on our own, picking a certain place to call home, a bin in a back street that had enough room for all seven of us growing kittens, and our mum, of course.

'Ty was always the leader, the boss. He liked to play-fight with the others, and show us his dominance through physical, if not mental, power. He was coal black, most probably the coat of our father, a cat we never and have still never seen, with two deadly amber eyes that we learned to fear.

'You see, playful dominance soon turned into all out violence and anger, especially after we came home one day to find our mother gone and a few greedy stray dogs in her place. Me and Sapphire ran to hide, while Ty tried to sort them out, but they didn't listen to him, for obvious reasons.

They toyed with him, giving him a few scars along the way, before leaving. That was what turned Ty sour. And that is why we have learnt to hate all dogs, any dogs at all.

'After that encounter, Ty took his anger out on his weaker litter-mates, namely Sapphire and another female called Eliza, or Liz for short. That is why Sapphire is always so quiet. He made sure we followed his every order, hunting every day just to fill his preposterous demands, and we were regularly told to sleep out on the street, just so he could have all the room in the bin to himself.

'But me and Sapphire soon got tired of his constant bullying, so one night we ran off and found ourselves all alone, sleeping under bins and on walls, sneaking into gardens and napping in the sheds; anywhere we could lie down, we called home. It was on one such occasion that the owner of the shed happened to come in and find us, but instead of shooing us away he brought us into his house and introduced us to his other cat, who we now know is called Shadow. We were given new names, and, subsequently, new lives. And that is our story."

Throughout Ruby's speech, Sapphire

only nodded and made slight agreeing noises, keeping quiet, and I now understand why. All this time, I had thought it better to keep the past hidden, and not to pry into other cat's (And dog's) business, although I did know a few of the key points in Ruby and Sapphire's story beforehand, from a few slipped words in our conversations. But now I know that the opposite is actually true. Now that we know more about each other, I think we can bond more, as friends. But, as I look from Ruby to Baxter, I also know that some grudges cannot be ended so easily.

But I still have hope. After all, Baxter still hasn't shared his past with us, and that story may swing Ruby's opinion of the highly spirited dog. But, there again, it may not. Ruby can be extremely stubborn when she wants to, and now is not an exception. She and Sapphire have always hated dogs, probably since the day they were born, as alleycats and stray dogs don't usually go together well, and lasting opinions are hard to change.

However, after that particularly long story, I know that Sophia is ready to sleep, so I suggest that everyone else heads to bed. They all agree, except for Baxter, whose claims that he is 'Not tired at all!' are quickly disregarded by Tess. I climb into my usual cardboard box, with Sophia coming in after me, and find myself slipping into a slumber easier than normal. But I don't try and stop it, I just wait until Sophia is sound asleep, which doesn't take long, as the young kitten must be extremely tired out from everything that has happened.

Closing my eyes, and finally letting my worn out body rest, I slowly slip into a pleasant, dreamless slumber, everything gradually turning black. And that's the way I like it.

Chapter Nine

"I forgot!!"

The loud barks and slight whines of Baxter wake both me and Sophia up, annoyingly. She looks at me sleepily, through tired eyes, and I recognise the look to be one of hunger.

"We'll have breakfast soon, Sophia." I promise her. "Once I've sorted this lunatic out."

She smiles slightly at my remark, before turning over and trying to get a few more minutes of sleep. I, however, have an uncontrollable dog to quiet down, and breakfast to find, so I jump out of the cardboard box and take in the chaotic scene before me.

Baxter is racing around, whining about forgetting something, while an annoyed Ruby, who has just woken up, is quietly talking with Sapphire. And, from what I can hear of the conversation, they don't exactly seem to be complimenting Baxter. But, there again, you can't blame Ruby for not taking to the exuberant dog, especially after years of fearing and despising the creature. Some cats just don't like to simply let things go.

"Baxter!" I walk over to where the dog has stopped to finally rest. "What's the problem?"

"I forgot!" He cries, as if he thinks it is extremely obvious.

"I got that far." I sigh; every single conversation with Baxter is a struggle. "What exactly have you forgotten?"

"I was going to tell everyone why dogs are so amazing!"

Oh. I remember now. I told him that he should tell everyone why he thinks dogs are so amazing, and he took it a little too seriously. Well, it can't turn out too bad, although I am extremely surprised that he was so upset about such a little thing. Personally, I wouldn't have even bothered about it, maybe felt a little unsatisfied by the fact that I had forgotten, but nothing more. There again, I am certainly not Baxter.

"Well... you can tell them tonight, can't you?" I offer.

"Oh... yeah, I can! Thanks Shadow!"

The young dog races off, probably to find Tess, as they are never far apart. I really cannot even begin to understand him. He seemed so tough, so aggressive, when we first saw him, but now? Everything's changed. We now see the side of him that no one else sees, the childlike, innocent, enthusiastic, if easily excitable, side of him, and that's what truly matters. I guess he's just not really one for first impressions.

But Ruby still hasn't even started to warm up to him, and that's what worries me. If Joseph never comes back, which I am sad to say is the most likely possibility, then I can't have two members of my Tribe - as I now count Baxter as one of my Tribe, thanks to his recent actions of kindness towards all of us - constantly arguing and bickering. It's the last thing anyone needs in their tribe, but in our situation? Everyone needs to stick together now more than ever. And I know that Baxter is willing to be friendly towards both Ruby and Sapphire, but Ruby is too biased in her opinion of dogs in general (Bar Tess) and he still frightens Sapphire, even with his quietest bark, due to her past experiences. It's the worst possible situation that we could be in.

I have a feeling, however, that Baxter's story this evening might make Ruby less hostile towards him. But that all depends on what Baxter plans to tell us. I'm guessing he wants to tell us why dogs are so good, in his eyes, but he will probably include some of his past in this as well. It's amazing how much we have all learnt about each other in a matter of days, when we have spent years together but never spoke a word about our past. Well, with the exception of Tess, obviously.

When I think about it, it seems to be Tess that has brought us all together. Tess' telling of her past made everyone feel safer and more inclined to tell their own stories, which in turn made us all know more about each other than ever before. Tess, the latest addition to our household, has also been one of the most useful members of my Tribe, and for that I am extremely grateful.

But, relationship trouble aside, everyone will be even grumpier, and Ruby even more short tempered, if they don't receive breakfast. And that essential task is in the paws of our very own Baxter. Which is why it is almost certainly guaranteed to go very, very wrong.

"Baxter!" I call, heading into the Living Room, to see him curled up by the side of Tess.

"Yeah?" He replies, as enthusiastic as ever, jumping up at the sound of my voice, as Tess chuckles at his antics.

"Sorry to bother you, but we need

71

breakfast, and you seem to be the only animal here who is able to deliver it."

"Certainly!" He grins, running into the Kitchen, and the sounds of a can smashing against the wall tell me that he's doing his job.

"Boundless energy, that pup." Tess smiles.

"You're telling me!" I laugh, following the sounds of destruction into the Kitchen.

The scene I see before me is one of complete and utter pandemonium. The Twins' fortress has been toppled, Ruby is scolding Baxter with harsh words and eyes that look ready to kill, and Sapphire is hiding underneath a mountain of cat-food cans. Hiding or stuck, I wonder grimly, walking over to the cat-food can that caused all the trouble. The top has burst open, and its smell is so enchanting that Sophia has woken up and is peeking over the top of the cardboard box, while Tess has come in from the Living-Room.

When Ruby sees me, she stops scolding Baxter and instead explains to me what has happened.

"This... oaf," She starts, her face more frustrated and angry than I have ever seen it before, "Decided to take one of the bottom tins from our den! And it fell! And he crashed into it too! And he didn't care!"

"I did care!" Baxter protests. "I just needed to make everyone breakfast!"

"And ruin our den!" She retorts, temper flaring. "Then, he says it isn't his fault!"

"It wasn't! I didn't know it would collapse! And I didn't mean to fall into it!"

"You did! All dogs ever do is get in the way and ruin things for cats! That's how it's always been, and nothing's changed!"

With that last remark, Ruby stalks into the Living-Room, and Sapphire, having freed herself from the ruins of the once-fortress, now pile of cat-food cans, follows her quickly. Baxter looks so hurt that I feel quite sorry for him, and Tess goes over to comfort him quickly, but my top priority is Sophia. She ducked back into the cardboard box half way through that shouting match, and I need to make sure she's alright.

As I go into the Kitchen, I hear the last words of Tess and Baxter's conversation, before he goes to lie in a corner, upset and ashamed, and they are simply:

"I didn't get to tell everyone why dogs are amazing!"

"Another time, Baxter, another time."

But comforting the poor Baxter comes after making sure Sophia is ok, in my head, so I look into the cardboard box to see a shaking and visibly frightened Sophia. My words of reassurance do little to comfort her, but she does finally agree, with a nod of her head, to come out of the box, and we walk through the Kitchen then into the Living-Room together. It is only then that I realise an eerie silence has befallen the entire house, the tip of Sapphire's tail on the stairs telling me that the Twins' have gone upstairs to seek solitude, so me and Sophia are alone in the Living-Room.

But, as we curl up together on the seat of the Armchair, I can't help but wish that everyone would just get along. Dogs will be dogs and cats will be cats, but can't we just be ourselves and at least like each other?

As the day has only just started, and it is, for once, quite warm, I decide that me and Sophia can rest on the Armchair, for a little while, just in case Joseph decides to come back. It's still possible, and I don't care what anyone says. Joseph could just walk in right now, even though it's unlikely. And I don't want to give up hope, because hope is what keeps you going through the coldest nights and the darkest days. Sometimes, hope is all you have left.

Sophia closes her eyes, but I highly doubt that she is sleeping. Probably just relaxing, thinking over things, like the argument. I feel so sorry for her, having to live through this, without Joseph as well. Being alone, without your parents, on the streets, is bad, but being in an abandoned house with a volatile cat and her highly energetic rival might just be worse.

So, as the day wears on, not much happens. Me and Sophia go into the Kitchen, where Baxter is timidly trying (And failing) to rebuild the Twins' fortress, Tess licking half-heartedly at a tin of cat-food, but she stops when we come in, batting the tin over to us. Sophia is quick to eat some, as am I, since breakfast was delayed for quite a while, and afterwards I debate whether I should go up and talk to Ruby or not. Finally, I decide against it, reasoning that Sapphire can always calm her down. They have been up there a long time, though, so I decide to bring them some food if they stay upstairs for too much longer.

Sophia and I spend the rest of the day

either lounging on the Armchair or in the Kitchen, helping to reconstruct the Twins' fortress. Baxter has put in a lot of effort, but he keeps knocking it down accidentally, so it takes a while. But, by the time the evening draws near, the fortress is almost back to how it used to look, and I take an opened can of cat-food upstairs, finding Ruby and Sapphire asleep on the bedroom floor. Instead of waking them, I just leave the food by them, but Sapphire wakes up at the quiet sound of the can hitting the floor, nods at me, then goes back to sleep.

I return to the Living-Room, where Tess and Sophia are lying by Baxter's den, and Baxter is telling some sort of story. By the time I get over there, he has stopped, and smiles at me.

"Shadow!" He says, with all the eagerness he lost this morning recovered. "I'm telling everyone why dogs are amazing!"

"Do you mind if we listen?" A voice comes from near the stairs, and we all turn to see Ruby and Sapphire, walking towards us slowly.

"Uh... no?" Baxter offers, as Ruby nods, lying down with Sapphire by her side.

"Good. Start the story."

76

Ruby's frosty tones may seem to represent resentment towards Baxter, but I know Ruby, and she means well. There is no formal apology, but, as Baxter launches into his story, I sense that all is forgiven. And I'm right. But what caused Ruby's sudden change of heart is a mystery to me, and everyone else, although I am truly grateful for it. I have a sneaky feeling, however, in the back of my mind, which says that Sapphire has something to do with it... if that feeling is right, then I can't say that I'm surprised. I really can't.

Chapter Ten

"Dogs," Baxter starts, pausing for a little thought, before continuing, "Are amazing, because we're good fun. There's few dogs out there that'll say no to a game of fetch, isn't there ma?"

"There is indeed." Tess confirms.

"So we're always good for playing games. That means we're amazing because you're never bored around us. We're always causing fun things to happen!"

"And mischief." Tess adds, with a small smile.

"And mischief." Baxter nods. "Like when me and my brothers and my one sister went to steal our owner's hat, it was so funny! She was all posh, you see, so you'd think she'd like poodles or something, but no! Us! My ma - real ma, that is, not you Tess, but you're still a really good ma - went mad at us afterwards, but it was worth it! The hat had all funny flowers on it too, but they tasted horrible! Ugh!"

Everyone chuckles at that last remark, even Ruby. Baxter is well known for eating (Or, at least, trying to eat) pretty much everything, and I can certainly imagine that a hat would be no exception.

"Of course, we always had good fun

with our owner too, chasing the little Chi-whatsit around, the one that sat in her handbag all day. What's it called ma?"

"A Chihuahua." Tess corrects him patiently.

"Yeah, a Chihuahua. Well, it didn't like us, but it was tiny anyway, so we were always chasing it around. But it didn't ever snap at us, which is another reason why we're amazing: most of us don't do aggressive stuff. Isn't that right ma?"

"It is indeed." Tess nods. "And a good thing too."

"Yeah, because we're so much good fun, no one wants to do aggressive stuff. Except the ones that aren't good fun... but they're just mean, right ma?"

"Yes, Baxter, very mean."

"Nothing like most of us, anyway. I was never mean, and I'm still not mean, am I?"

All of us shake our heads, Tess saying 'Of course not!'. Who could possibly think that Baxter is mean? He's as nice, friendly and polite as they come, although he could do with being a little less energetic at times. Just a little bit. Baxter is glancing at Ruby with an almost fearful look, as if he thinks her reply will be negative, but she sends him a reassuring one back, so he sighs in relief and starts up his story again.

"I suppose now would be a good time to tell you all my story, right?"

We all nod, and he smiles, continuing.

"Right, so, I was born in this big house, with my real ma and my dad, and my brothers, and my one sister, and the Chihua-watsit. Oh yeah, and our owner, this posh lady. We lived there for ages, playing and eating and sleeping and playing and eating and eating... well, you get it.

'But then we got older. Bigger. The lady started telling us off for things, even things that weren't us, whacking our noses with a rolled up newspaper when we even enjoyed ourselves! So we just acted all nice, and happy, and stayed excitable, because... I suppose... we were just... avoiding the truth. That she didn't like us. She seemed to hate us. The older we got, the nastier she was, throwing us out the house when it was raining, into the back garden. Then my real ma... she... died. And my dad disappeared. And we were left all alone, out in the cold every night and with the lady everyday. It wasn't... nice. I didn't like it, my brothers didn't like it, and my sister didn't like it. It was horrible."

His face saddens at the memory, and I understand how he feels. It's the worst thing to ever experience, having an owner that doesn't like you. It's worse than being all alone, much worse. It's like waking up and just wanting to go back to sleep, because dreams are better than reality. But you have to get up, because there's just the chance that your owner might like you today, like they did on the day they got you, but they don't, and you spend the rest of the day wishing that you never got up, then the night is spent dreading the next day. It's just terrible.

"So, one day, when we got put out in the back garden, and we saw the gate was open, we went. Just like that. One by one, we all disappeared out into the street, walking down road after road, barking at anyone who tried to pick us up, or stroke us. But I know now why they went away, and didn't just keep bothering us. We were Staffies. Staffordshire Bull Terriers. We had a bad reputation, and all our barking did was confirm the rumours. People left us alone, but we stuck together. Always.

'Then came the day that they found us.

We were about one and a half years old, and they found us in a alleyway, and they caught us. They brought us to this big, scary place, then they did the worst thing ever. They... separated us."

Baxter whispers the last part, head down, the sadness overwhelming him. Tess rests her head on his back, her paws on his, murmuring words of encouragement to him, before he finally lifts his head back up, and continues telling his tale.

"I felt something, in that cage, that I'd never felt before. It felt all hot inside me, but not in a good way. I felt like I needed to rip something to pieces, or bite someone, just because they had took me away from my brothers and sister. I know it's called anger, now. But I'd never felt it before. Sadness, yes, happiness, yes, but anger? No. It felt wrong, but I couldn't get rid of it, so I lashed out at everything and everyone, including the man who took me out of the cage and into a car, then into a house with three cats and a small white thing. Sorry, I mean Sophia."

A small, bashful smile lights up his face, and Sophia meows quietly in his direction, possibly a 'It doesn't matter', but, like with Sapphire, you can never be too sure what

Sophia is saying.

"And now I'm here." He finishes. "And that's why dogs are amazing."

After that... interesting story, the darkness has totally engulfed the Living-Room, so we all decide to go and sleep. Like every night, Sophia follows me to my den, and we curl up with the blankets inside it. But tonight, unlike many other nights, sleep comes easily, taking over my exhausted mind with a single push. The argument must have been what wore me out, I think, and the last thing I hear is the gentle sound of Sophia's breathing, before tiredness floods into my mind, and I am asleep.

"Shush!" Someone mutters, as I slowly wake up, shaking my head to get rid of a groggy feeling that I don't usually have when I get up. I must have really been tired last night.

"You'll wake everyone up!" The same voice, a little louder, says, but my sleepy mind can't work out who it is.

"Sorry!" This voice I recognise immediately: Baxter.

"Whatever, just come on!"

I have a feeling that the first voice is Ruby, but I'm not sure, and why would they be up so early? And is Sapphire there? Sapphire goes wherever Ruby goes, so it's unlikely that they'll be apart.

Shaking my head slightly (And praying that Baxter doesn't break anything important) I turn over and see Sophia still asleep. Actually, I should be asleep too, as there is only a slight light coming into the room, which means it is very early morning. Time to sleep.

So I try to, but it's hard. Thoughts whirl around my head, renewed by however many hours of sleep I got, mostly of Ruby and Baxter. Ruby is not a strange cat, just a constantly changing one. One day, she's extremely hot headed and short tempered, the next? She's back to being the nice, if protective, cat we all know well. Ruby isn't strange, just unpredictable.

And then there's Baxter. Baxter isn't strange either, but you do need an entire other category for him. Excitable is a major understatement. Mental comes close. But I can't be hard on him. The dog's been through a lot, so it's only natural that he has turned out a bit... different to everyone else, I suppose you could say.

While some dogs can control their

longing for 'good fun', as Baxter puts it, he can't even try to take it down a notch, let alone act normal. But that dog brings a smile to my face faster than anything else in the world, and that's an achievement he should be proud of.

The only thing in the world that even comes close is Sophia, and there's a clear reason why. Seeing her smile makes me smile immediately, seeing her happy makes me happy, and seeing her sad makes me sad. I do everything to fill the role that Snowdrop left for me, the role of Sophia's protector, and I hope I do it well. Maybe she's looking down on me, from the Cat Heaven up in the sky, and she's smiling too. I dearly hope so. Snowdrop was a wonderful cat, possibly the nicest stray you'd ever meet. When she died, my heart broke, and it stayed broken, until I met Sophia, for the second time. She has been slowly healing me ever since. And, next to Snowdrop, Sophia is the most important cat in my life.

It is with these content thoughts settled in my mind that I close my eyes and start to doze, the peculiar conversation from before almost completely forgotten, replaced by distant dreams that I can't quite figure out the meaning to, but I'm sure that they're not nightmares. Most are just muddles of confused and unrecognisable colours, like you see through the window in the kitchen, but every now and again I recognise a faint face, or a muffled voice, and that makes me feel a little bit better about the weird dream, giving me a strange sense of not being alone.

I must have fallen asleep, as the loud, and very clear, sound of Ruby's voice suddenly rings through my head, and the entire house. My eyes dart open, seeing that Sophia has suddenly woken, as I have, and we both listen to Ruby's call.

"Everyone come to the Living-Room! We've got a surprise for you!"

Chapter Eleven

"Come on, Sophia," I say, less tired than when I first woke up, "Let's go and see what on earth they're on about."

She nods, still sleepy, following me as I jump out of my den then scampering after me as I climb the mountain of rubbish that leads to the Living-Room. Once I've slid down, I look up, to see Ruby, Sapphire and Baxter in front of the T.V, all looking incredibly proud of themselves. Tess is also there, but she looks very tired, and is lying in her usual spot by the Armchair, but not on it. As I enter, Ruby grins and walks over to me.

"Shadow!" She exclaims. "Baxter had an idea, well, I helped him, and so did Sapphire, so..."

"What exactly are you doing?" I ask, curious.

"We think we can get the T.V working!" Baxter hurriedly explains.

"How?"

"The remote! It controls the T.V, which means, if you press the right button, it turns on!"

"Have you tried it yet?"

"We've tried every single button except the big red one at the top, because I thought it looked sinister at first, but now it has to be that one!" Ruby sounds so confident, I can't help but be a little bit excited.

"So... when are you planning on trying it?"

"Now! Everyone get to the Armchair!"

I leap up to my place at the top of the Armchair, Sophia sitting in her middle spot, the Twins on the arms of the Armchair, Ruby with the remote. The dogs are lying at the bottom of the Armchair, and the anticipation can be felt in the air. We haven't watched T.V since Joseph was here, and that... that seems like such a long time ago.

It seems like years since he struggled with the taps everyday, even though we all knew that no water ever came out. When he opened the tins of cat food with a strange metal contraption, and poured it into our bowls with ease. When we all fell asleep surrounding him on the Armchair, the T.V still on, playing quietly in the background of our dreams. All that is gone, now. But we're slowly getting it back, and although getting the T.V working is just one step in the right direction, it is a very big step. If it works, that is.

Ruby carefully presses the red button with her paw, head snapping up when the

T.V makes a static sound, then a sound like it is coughing and groaning, then finally splutters as a picture comes on the screen, of some sort of very clean kitchen, and people cooking. The words 'Saturday Morning Kitchen Live' are on the screen too, which is how I suddenly know that it is Saturday. Everyone cheers, Baxter barking excitedly, Sophia smiling in excitement.

The people on the T.V are the first humans we have seen in ages, and they look nothing like Joseph. In fact, they don't even look like the busy, boring people I saw on the streets, when I didn't have a home. They look... happy. Laughing and joking, like they have no worries. I never noticed it before, but now I look, the people on T.V are nothing like people when you meet them in real life. Or are they? It's been so long, since I went out on the streets, so maybe people have changed. I highly doubt it, but it's possible. Maybe they aren't so bad anymore, so grumpy all the time, especially when it's raining. But there again, maybe they've never changed. I have a feeling that is the more likely option, but you never know.

Within a few minutes of the T.V being turned on, though, something bad happens, predictably, to change the atmosphere of excitement and joy into one of annoyance and hostility. Baxter gets up, and Ruby hisses at him to get out of the way, since she can't see the T.V. But he takes no notice of her, instead going into a crouch. Everyone is confused, and annoyed, as he is blocking the T.V, and Sophia even climbs up to the top of the Armchair, but if she does it so she can be with me or so she can see the T.V better is the question.

Finally, Baxter jumps, landing on the Armchair, startling Tess, who scrambles to get out of the way, and Ruby, who hisses and jumps out of the way, landing on some rubbish. Sapphire does the same, speeding around the back of the Armchair and hiding behind her Twin, as Ruby spits at Baxter. But the huge dog just curls up, settles down, and starts watching T.V like nothing has happened. Ruby, of course, is not having that. She goes to the remote and switches off the T.V, before turning on Baxter.

"Down. Now." Her voice is so menacing that I'm sure she's going to rip him to pieces if he doesn't do as she says.

"Why?" He whines. "It's comfy!"

"It's also not for dogs. So down."

"Come on! Please!" He cries.

"No! No dogs are allowed on the Armchair! No exceptions!"

"Please!"

"Baxter!" Tess sounds angry, which is a surprise to all of us. "Don't disgrace yourself, and get down from that Armchair now. A place like that is earned through trust and respect, not pure force! I am ashamed of you. Surely you know how much the Armchair means to the cats, how it symbolises their hope for Joseph coming back, and how it is such a special place for them. The only creatures that have ever sat on there are humans and cats, and that should be how it stays. A dog's place, I have to admit, is lower than a cat's in the household. We're not allowed on furniture, or in the Kitchen when meals are being served, or to even play fight with the cats, when humans are around. Nothing should change when humans aren't here. Remember that, if nothing else."

Her face is one of pure disappointment, and I can tell that she didn't want to say all that, but it was necessary. To be honest, I'm not one of those cats that openly supports the 'cats over dogs' rule, but it's there for a reason. And this is the reason. Sometimes, dogs just do unexplainable things, which even they can't see the point of, but cats always have reasons for everything. We lavish humans in affection because they are sure to give it back, and it's a way of thanking them for everything they do for us. We don't try the same thing with dogs, because they just don't understand our ways of showing love or gratitude, and most dogs are prepared to bite your head off if you even go in the same room as them. Not all dogs, but enough to make us cautious about every dog we meet.

Baxter hangs his head low in shame, dropping from the Armchair to the floor.

"I reckon..." Ruby starts. "There should be punishment for breaking the rules."

"Nothing too harsh." I add in quickly, making sure this doesn't go too far.

"No, nothing like that. Just... no T.V for the rest of today. And he has to go in his old room."

"Fine. You ok with this Baxter?" I look at the dog for confirmation, and he nods. I then look at Tess, as she sighs and nods as well, going with Baxter into the kitchen and returning a few moments later.

"He's in his room, and he won't come out for the rest of today. Because of the punishment or because of shame, though, I don't know." Tess shakes her head slowly, going back to her place in front of the Armchair and lying down. "I hate telling him off. But it was needed."

"I agree. He is like a kitten in a dog's body than an almost mature pup."

Everyone smiles weakly at that last remark, as Ruby turns the T.V back on and the Twins return to their places on the arms of the Armchair. But Sophia stays up on the top of the Armchair with me, as programme after programme starts and finishes. At one point, I get up and go through to the Kitchen, needing to stretch my legs, and spot a can of cat-food still up on a shelf. An idea springs into my mind, and I make my way up to the Shelf, before batting the can towards the edge, a final push making it fall to the ground, and it lands on some sort of metal, which makes a rip in the can's side. Late breakfast? Maybe I should just call it dinner.

I think that's a better idea, so I pour the food into each of our bowls, leaving some behind for Tess, and call out:

"Dinner!"

Ruby is the first through the doorway, Sapphire just after her, Sophia skipping over the rubbish before Tess walks in after them all, a weary smile on her face. I bat the tin over to her, explaining that I left some in for her, and she thanks me, eating it before going back to the Living-Room, saying that she's tired and needs to rest. I understand. Tess is an old dog, and gets tired easily. And all of us know that life is even harder without Joseph here to support and guide us. Hope is all we have left, sometimes. The feeling that Joseph is going to come back, and that he definitely still loves us. I refuse to believe that he has abandoned us. He would never do that. Ever.

After dinner is finished, everyone goes back into the Living-Room, and we see that Tess is asleep. I signal to everyone, telling them to be quiet, as we climb onto the Armchair and start watching a programme on the T.V. And, as I look around at my Tribe, I think that I'm lucky. It's better to not have an owner but still have your family, than to not have anyone at all. I think everyone can agree with that.

Chapter Twelve

A lot can happen in seven days. Food can start running out. Seven days of feeding two dogs and four cats can really deplete our supplies. And hope can be lost. Everyday, we wake up hoping to see Joseph, but every night we go to bed without him. Everyday, the tension between Ruby and Baxter threatens to suddenly snap, and Sophia grows older, while Tess becomes tired more often, and less determined to see Joseph again. It's as if she's slowly slipping away from us, and I can't do anything about it. But Baxter really isn't helping. He is now certain that Jospeh won't come back, and the feeling starts to rub off on everyone else. He's growing older, but wiser? Possibly not.

So today, as I struggle to force myself to get out of bed, the looming despair of Joseph not being there making itself at home in my mind, I think back to happier times. The time when Joesph adopted me, brought me home, fed me, kept me company, even through the coldest nights, never sent me out of the room, never told me off, spoke to me like a friend, not an owner... he would never even dream of leaving and not coming back. So there is a chance, a small chance, that he is through that doorway, dozing away in his Armchair, that he will make Baxter and Ruby see sense and stop arguing, that he will make Tess, Sophia and Sapphire happy again. They have both been rather quiet, Sophia following me around at all times and never leaving my side. It's as if she fears what will happen to her if I am not there. And I hate her having to feel like that.

Finally, I force myself to get up and jump out of my den. Sophia is still sleeping, and I feel a little bit bad about leaving her in there alone, but Sapphire and Ruby are still sleeping in here, in their fortress, so she won't exactly be alone.

I walk slowly into the Living-Room, an unbearable sadness overwhelming my body when I see that Joseph has still not returned. I don't know why, but, for a minute, I almost thought that today would be the day. That Joseph would just be sitting there, maybe sleeping, maybe watching the T.V, maybe stroking Tess, or just staring into space. But he isn't here. He's never here. Everyday, I walk through the same doorway and feel exactly the same feeling. Sadness. Maybe even neglect, but mostly sadness. And maybe disappointment. Today, of all days, I really thought he would be back. I made myself believe that he would be here, but he isn't. Like usual.

Baxter snores lightly, turning over in his sleep, before grunting and moving his legs a little bit, then turning back over. I wonder what he's dreaming about. Probably chasing rabbits, or something else that dogs love to do. Something irrelevant, that acts like an escape from the real world. From the horrors of finding out that we're running out of food, or that we could be stuck in here, without Joseph, forever. That we could die here.

But there's no point moaning about something that could happen. It's not definite, so it might not happen. If it doesn't happen, then I will have been worrying about nothing, and everything will be ok. However, there's always the possibility that it will happen, in which case none of us will be ok, but my worrying won't help anyway.

I suppose, then, that I should just stop worrying and enjoy life at the moment, but that's near-impossible. We're running out of food, Baxter gets grumpy every time he's asked to help out with meals, and the Twins' fortress is now just a few cans standing around a bundle of blankets and old clothes.

You probably have already guessed that Ruby is not at all happy with this development, and primarily blames Baxter. This, of course, usually ends in arguments, that, in turn, end with either Ruby stalking off upstairs, Sapphire in tow, or Baxter going off to sulk in his room, and I don't know which outcome I prefer.

The only time that this house is ever peaceful is very early in the morning and very late at night. Those are the times when I like to take a walk around the rooms, to gather my thoughts and try to think of solutions to seemingly inevitable problems. That is the job of a Tribe leader, after all. To sort out conflicts and think of ways to solve problems. At the moment, I don't think I'm capable of either. Ruby and Baxter will never stop arguing, and sooner or later one of them is going to snap, and a fight is going to occur. I'm just hoping that day isn't coming too soon, because I don't think Ruby, with all her claws and teeth, can stop an angry Baxter.

To be honest, I thought that Ruby had forgiven him completely, and that no grudges remained, but that obviously isn't the case. I feel sorry for Sapphire, Sophia and

Tess too, but mostly Sapphire. She follows her twin everywhere, and has to listen to all the arguing, barking, hissing and spitting that goes on. Day in, day out, Ruby and Baxter will argue all the time, over the smallest of things. And there's nothing we can say or do to stop them.

I sigh. The early morning sun is reaching in through the window, as if it wants to reassure me that everything will be alright, someday. Yeah, I like to believe that. But is it true? That I just cannot say. So I do what I always do, early in the morning, to take my mind off things. I go up to the window sill in the Kitchen, and I sit there, letting my mind wander aimlessly, even if it is only a way to pass the hours. Those endless, mind-numbing hours, when there is nothing to do but talk about the exact same things, listen to Ruby complain about Baxter, listen to Baxter complain about Ruby, and think. Thinking seems to take up most of my time now.

Not that I didn't do it before, but now it seems so much more important to me, carefully going through all the problems we are facing and trying to solve them while pretending to have a nap. The nap part is very important, by the way, so the others don't pester me about why I am just staring into space. I know they mean well, and they just want to check that I'm alright, but it gets irritating very quickly, and I definitely don't want to turn into my old self and just snap at everyone. Definitely not.

But how do I solve the problems? First is the problem of food. We're going to starve, if we don't find some sort of food source that isn't rats (Who have practically disappeared), mice (Who have disappeared) or cat-food (Which is all but gone), and quickly too. Then there's Ruby and Baxter. If that first problem is hard, then this one is impossible. There's no way to force them to like each other, and get along, or I would have done it by now, trust me. Everyone's sick of the constant quarreling, including me, and sooner or later, someone's going to get hurt. It's unavoidable. And, when everyone goes hungry again, because we've ran out of food, the two will be even more grumpy and irritable, so a fight is even more likely to break out.

I really don't get what I'm meant to do. It's like the Tribe is falling apart. We're down to our last cans of cat-food, so it's one a day until we can find a different food source. I'm going to tell Sapphire and Ruby to focus on hunting, and maybe they can teach Sophia a thing or two. Any help is good help. Well, as long as Baxter doesn't start to 'help' only to rile up Ruby, who will promptly stop hunting and start arguing, and even less rats will be caught. That means less food. And I can't let that happen. Ever.

But food doesn't just appear out of nowhere. The rats and mice need to eat, so, if they have nothing left to nibble on, they'll relocate, and leave us to starve. Human food is mostly inaccessible or even rotten, in some cases. So what do we do?

I don't know. But I do know that, while I've been sitting on this window sill, almost everyone else has woken up. I can hear Baxter padding around the Kitchen, and Ruby talking to Sapphire in the Living-Room. I can even hear the gentle breathing of a sleeping Sophia, and that reminds me of why I keep going. Why I don't just give up and tell everyone to solve their own problems. Because of her. I need to stay strong, and loyal to the Tribe, so that Sophia can grow up properly, and so that she doesn't have to be afraid of everything, because I'm here. She's the center of my world, and if I were to lose her, I would lose everything.

That is why I need to find food. It doesn't matter what it is, or where it comes from; as long as it's edible and will fill hungry stomachs, it's fine. Then there's Ruby and Baxter. I could just separate them as much as possible, but a fight is inevitable. Instead of pushing it away, I should probably figure out what I'm going to do when the time comes. Stop the fight? That's the obvious choice. I don't want anyone getting hurt, be it Baxter, Ruby or an innocent bystander.

But there is a downside to stopping it. Several, actually. For starters, I might not be able to stop it. Some fights spiral out of control extremely quickly, and, before you know it, someone is gravely injured and the winner is turning on the crowd, in some sort of frenzy that is fuelled by the adrenaline of winning a fight... trust me, I've seen it before. And it is not pretty.

Then there's another thing to consider: no fight means no satisfaction. The grudge will go on, and that means even more arguments than before. I just don't know what I should do. Everything is much more complicated when you don't have an owner to work things out for you, but I suppose it's just part of life now. And besides, Joseph is bound to come back soon... right? I'm just getting worried, because it's been more than a week since he left, and the thought that he could have abandoned us is playing heavily on my mind. I just hope that he hasn't. He wouldn't. He couldn't. Could he?

Chapter Thirteen

"Stupid dog! I've had it with you!"

"Me too! But you're a cat!"

Ferocious barks and yowls make me look around quickly, my eyes fixing on a scene in the Living-Room that I will never forget. It makes me hurry to jump off the window sill and race towards the doorway, only stopping to peek into the cardboard box and quickly tell Sophia to stay put, as she has been woken up by all the noise, before leaping over the mountain of rubbish that guards the Living-Room to find Baxter and Ruby circling each other, snarling and spitting. Sapphire is hiding behind Tess, who is begging Baxter to stop it, but he isn't listening. Neither is Ruby, unfortunately, so their insults grow more and more tormenting, both of them completely powered by rage and resentment, built up from weeks of hating each other. It's horrible. Just horrible.

Then they stop. And that signals the start of the fight. Ruby crouches down, claws at the ready. Baxter opens his jaws, displaying two rows of knife-like teeth. Ruby has her eyes locked onto her target. There is no noise at all in the house. Only silence. Then she strikes. A fearsome yowl erupts from her throat, as she flies forwards, almost imitating the move that Sapphire used a long time ago, to catch a rat in the Living-Room. That was such a long time ago... But there is no time to dwell on the matter, as Ruby's claws almost tear at Baxter's shoulder, but miss by a milimetre as Baxter moves quickly to dodge the attack. Suddenly, Baxter jumps at Ruby, jaws darting forwards to try and grab her, most probably by the neck, but she is already gone, speeding away from the dog, almost taunting him. Not a good idea.

"You stupid cat!" He growls, charging towards her, but I quickly take this chance to jump at him myself.

We roll for a few seconds, both demanding to win the fight, before I finally gain the upper hand and end up on top of the huge dog. Somehow, I have kept his jaws away from me, and the only injury I have is a small scratch from one of his claws, that caught me by surprise. But, now that I am in control, I take the moment to try to talk some sense into him.

"Listen to me, Baxter. Now." My voice must be as menacing as I want it to sound, as Baxter whines a little, going ever so slightly limp, but still struggling quite a lot.

"I've won a dozen fights, probably more, and I don't care to add this to the non-existent list of fights I've lost. So give up now, and we can stop this idiotic feud once and for all."

"Yeah right!" He snaps, finally pushing me off him as we circle each other, me taking slow and deliberate steps, sizing up the beast carefully.

Ruby has gone back to Sapphire, and the two are staying behind Tess, out of the way. When she sees me looking, Ruby just nods at me, and I understand. She knows what I was like on the streets.

I was rough. Saying that is an extreme understatement. Not one male cat went by unchallenged, not one female wasn't scared away, not one dog passed who didn't then flee with his tail between his legs. I was your typical alleycat, a grumpy creature with a short temper and a stone heart. Humans thought I was a nuisance, dogs thought I was a menace, and the other cats just knew to stay away. I never lost a single fight. I also thought I'd never change. But then, out of the blue, Snowdrop comes walking into my life, and everything changes. You know the story from there.

I've challenged many a dog that was

bigger, and most certainly stronger, than Baxter, but his attitude is much more determined. Less... clever. More brash. As we circle each other, I realise that he'll be looking for a quick win, as to not waste too much of his energy. After all, he's definitely been affected the most by not having enough food, so, instead of also opting for the quick bite to the neck, I decide to drag things out a little. Once he's tired, I can then regain control of the battle, assert my dominance very clearly, then make sure that Ruby and Baxter see each other as little as possible afterwards.

I wait patiently for him to make his move. For my plan to work, I need to keep dodging and ducking, making sure that I don't just go straight in for a few nips then come out very sore and a loser. No way. That's how a dog fights. A dog, or a very stupid cat. And, predictably, Baxter attacks just like your average dog. A bark, to announce the attack (Mistake number one: surprise is everything), then he lunges at me (Mistake number two: lunges are easy for a cat to dodge). I move out of the way and watch as he crashes into the Armchair, suppressing a laugh. Focus. Need to focus.

No time for jokes.

The dog stands up again, rearing to go, flying at me with such speed that I am almost impressed. Almost. I dodge again, this time jumping up onto the T.V for protection, but I miss my footing and come tumbling down again, just so happening to land on Baxter's back - oh, the irony - feet first, claws out. Hey, not every fall has to look accidental!

He lets out a roar of pain, making me wonder for a minute if he turns into a lion when he's angry, before I reach down and swipe at one of his front legs. This makes him fall, rather ungracefully, to the floor, and I take the chance to declare the fight won. By me, of course. Ok, the victory was unexpected, as well as really quick, and none of it went as planned, but at least I won. Now to try and knock (Literally, if needed) some sense into the brash young Staffie.

"Baxter, there's no point fighting anymore. I've won, and that's that." I start, pleased to see that he's stopped struggling and seems to be listening, the fire in his eyes burning out very quickly, and exhaustion setting in. "We're all tired, and hungry, and I understand that you and Ruby will probably never get along."

"Ever!" Ruby calls, still behind Tess.

"Enough, Ruby. You're just as much to blame." Believe it or not, I am actually trying to be fair, and Baxter certainly isn't the only animal here who is in the wrong. "Anyway, my point is that, from now on, you two need to stop hating each other. A mutual dislike is fine by me, but your constant arguing and fighting is not what we need in times like these. Hope and hate have never went together, and they still don't. You already sleep in separate rooms, so I don't have to restrict you to those rooms all the time, do I?"

"No." They both mutter, sounding ashamed.

"Good. Now, I believe that we all need food. Hunting would be appreciated..."

"We're on it." Ruby interrupts me, as both she and Sapphire go over to a rat hole and start to catch dinner.

"Also, I need to check up on our supplies again. We must eat as little cat-food as possible. Tess, you can get some rest if you want. I also need to see Sophia."

"I'll start collecting the cans!" Baxter says excitedly, as I get off him and follow him into the Kitchen.

I look into the cardboard box to see a sleeping Sophia. She must have dozed off while waiting for me to come back. It's probably best for her to get as much sleep as possible, so I leave her to her dreamworld and return to Baxter, who tells me that we have a grand total of five cat-food cans. Not good.

I then turn to the cupboards. If I have searched them once then I have searched them a thousand times, but each search reveals new packets and cans, and even some dishes once, so I want to check again. Some things, like pasta, taste disgusting because we can't cook them like Joseph does. Well, did. I mean... ugh, this is so hard. I really, really want him to come back, and I never give up hoping, but is it really possible? Could he just walk in and act like nothing has ever happened? And if he did, what would happen to Baxter? Now that's something I haven't considered before. It's scary to think that we have been surviving for so long without our owner. Other cats wouldn't stand a chance. But we're different. Very different.

After a few minutes of scouring the

cupboards, I finally find a can of tuna and some mouldy bread. Deciding to leave the bread, I call over Baxter and he takes the tuna into the living room, where we all share it, after I wake up a sleepy Sophia and explain that dinner is ready. By the way, sharing tuna is very hard, because tuna cans just happen to be tiny. It makes no sense! Luckily, we have two rats to go with it, and a programme that makes no sense to us on the T.V, which we all watch anyway, Ruby watching Baxter carefully to make sure that he doesn't try to get on the Armchair again! But, overall, it is a successful meal, considering the fact that we are almost out of food and that means that we could starve to death very soon.

However, I know we'll find a way. We always do. Cats are survivors, and dogs aren't so bad at surviving either. We just need to work together, and we'll get through this. But working together is the hard part, especially with cats and dogs. I really have my work cut out for me, don't I?

Chapter Fourteen

Time goes slowly, crawling along, rather like a snail. Especially when you have nothing to do. After the commotion of this afternoon, the evening is quite uneventful, so Tess goes to sleep early. Baxter also decides to go and lie down in his den, so there are no more arguments between him and Ruby, thankfully. Instead, we turn off the T.V and decide to talk for a bit, just us four cats, but I suspect that Sophia is going to doze off soon.

We are sitting on the Armchair, but, instead of being in our usual places, we are all together on the middle part of the chair, Sophia curling into me and Sapphire lying just behind Ruby.

"Joseph isn't back yet." Ruby says bluntly, as Sapphire quietly grooms her twin.

"No." I answer quickly. "But that doesn't mean he won't come back soon."

"It's possible. But not likely. Not at this point." She replies.

"It could still happen. Anything is possible." I counter. She shrugs.

"But will it happen?" There is silence for a few minutes, as Sapphire murmurs in Ruby's ear, and Ruby nods her head slightly. "Sapphire says... she says we need to keep believing. Believing that he will come back."

"Because he will." I am adamant about that point.

"Yes, maybe."

We continue to talk about random subjects for a while, the darkness of night creeping into the Living-Room, as Baxter snores and Sophia finally goes to sleep. I suggest that we should do the same, and the Twins agree, so I lie down next to Sophia and shut my eyes, the room soon sliding into a thick silence, which is only broken every so often, by Baxter's snores. With everything and everyone fine, I find it easy to welcome sleep, and drift off to dreamland with ease.

When I wake up, it is still dark. But something is wrong. Usually, I can hear the breathing of all six of the animals in my Tribe, including myself. But today, I can only hear five, and I can identify them all. Myself, first, then the quiet breathing of Sophia, who is still sleeping next to me. The Twins are almost indistinguishable from each other, but Sapphire's breathing is just a fraction quieter than Ruby's. Then there's Baxter, who is still snoring. But Tess? I'm frightened, a little, because I can sense something that I usually only feel after a serious fight with another cat, and not anywhere else (And this fight was most probably with another male cat, when we were fighting for dominance a long time ago). It is the presence of death.

I immediately fear for Tess, for several reasons. She's the oldest, and the only animal who's breathing I can't hear, and... maybe I shouldn't be so quick to conclusions. Maybe I should just go back to sleep, and wake up, and everything will be alright. That is the naive approach, but there is a chance that this could all be a dream. There again, the entire situation with Joseph going missing could also be a dream, but I find that extremely unlikely. For many reasons. Such as it's length, and just because it all seems to be so real. Why shouldn't I trust my instincts? A cat goes by three things, its instincts, common sense and general knowledge. My instincts tell me that everything is fine, my common sense says I should wait until the morning to sort things out, and my general knowledge just isn't helping at this moment in time. Oh well; I suppose my only option is to wait.

An hour later, the sun starts to rise into the sky, pushing light slowly through the window in the Living-Room and waking up

Sapphire, who freezes instantly and looks towards Tess, then back at me, fear in her eyes. So it's not just me being paranoid. She slowly recovers from her temporary paralysis and wakes up Ruby, who has the same reaction. But she, after looking at me, quickly glances at Sophia, checking that she's still sleeping. I nod, before gesturing to Baxter with a flick of my tail. Ruby shrugs, hopping off the Armchair and approaching Tess, who is lying where she always used to sleep - on the floor in front of the Armchair - before sniffing the air, then turning to me and shaking her head. Refusing to believe what Ruby is telling me, I decide to check for myself, jumping off the Sofa and landing on the ground with a light thud. Sniff. The usual smell of rubbish, old food and dog (Ugh, horrible) is presented to my nose, but there is another smell in there too. Death, again. And it's more powerful this time, like a punch to the nose. Tess... is dead.

Sapphire makes a sort of crying noise, leaping off the Armchair and hiding behind Ruby. Of course, like everything Sapphire does, it's very quiet, but Sophia still wakes up, and I jump up onto the Armchair, wondering if I should explain everything to her. It will probably be best if I do.

"What's... that smell?" She asks quietly.

"...Tess..." I think desperately of how to word this. "Isn't... with us... anymore."

"She's... dead?" Sophia practically whispers the last part, eyes wide.

"Yes, I'm sorry Sophia." I sigh. Ruby and Sapphire come to my rescue, thankfully.

"But she's very happy." Ruby adds, as Sapphire whispers in her ear. "In dog heaven. Where all old dogs go after a while."

"Is it a nice place?"

"Yes, extremely nice. There's food, and toys..."

I jump off the Armchair, going into the Kitchen and up to my window sill, hearing Ruby tell Sophia all about 'Dog Heaven' and also briefly mentioning 'Cat Heaven'. Ruby can always calm down the young kitten, but I'm not so sure about Baxter. Tess is - or, I suppose, was - the only animal on earth who could calm him down, and now she's gone... I'm still processing the fact that she won't come back. It doesn't feel real.

The thing is, when I lived on the streets, there was death almost everywhere. The rats and mice you caught for food, the cats you fought for territory, and anyone who fell foul of the stray dog packs. But living in a house makes you forget all of that. You forget seeing every single other animal as either prey or a threat, making split second decisions to fight or flee, and the ache of your paws after days of travelling, not being able to stop anywhere because the humans just shoo you onwards. You are not wanted anywhere, so you just keep going. For some, it is until they die, but I was lucky enough to end up getting taken in by an animal shelter, then adopted. However, others are not so fortunate.

As I think, I calm down. But being calm never lasts long in this house, and, as expected, a pain-filled howl soon interrupts my thoughts. The second one is even sadder than the first, telling everyone of sorrow and grief, and each one rips into my heart. No dog, or cat, no matter what they have done, deserves to go through the heartache of losing a loved one, especially when that loved one is the closest to family that they've had for years. I don't think I can even face Baxter, but I force myself to stop running away from the problems and face up to them. Tess is gone. So it is imperative that we are there for him now, in his greatest time of need. That doesn't just mean Ruby and Sapphire. That means me too. I must help him. I have to.

With quite a bit of mental effort, I finally persuade myself to go through to the Living-Room, seeing a heart-broken Baxter still howling over the body of Tess. Emotions flash through my head, mostly pity and misery, but then another feeling flows into my mind, one that is much stronger than any other. It is determination.

"Baxter." I say softly, walking over to the dog and putting one of my paws on his.

"It's my fault!" His voice cries out, and I am surprised.

"Why on earth would it be your fault?" I ask, ever so slightly confused. "It's no one's fault. Everyone's time comes, and Tess' was now. You couldn't have stopped it."

"It was the fight!" He continues, so grief-stricken that I don't think he is even acknowledging me. "It shocked her, and this happened!"

"I'm sure it wasn't." I try to console him, but the thought that the fight could have been a factor in Tess' death is new to me. Could it be true?

"But... are you sure?" He finally seems to

notice me, and I nod enthusiastically at the upset dog.

"Very sure. Now, I'm not sure you want to talk about it, but we can't just... leave her here. Can we?"

"No. Definitely not." He shakes his head. "But we can't go outside or anything! The front door is locked and the back door is bordered up!"

"Who said we have to take her outside? I think I know just the place. But it will involve someone carrying her..."

"I'll do it. Where are you thinking?" He still has an air of sadness and grieving around him, but my encouragement seems to have done the trick, as he is in a slightly better mood than before.

"Upstairs, under the covers of the double bed. So she can rest in peace, and comfort."

He nods his approval, before looking down despairingly at Tess. Without a word, he lowers himself down, and I take the hint, attempting to roll Tess onto his back. Sapphire, astonishingly, also comes over to help, while Ruby is busy with Sophia. As Tess is quite light, we soon get her on Baxter's back, and I lead everyone upstairs, pondering over what on earth I should say when we get there.

After what seems like an age, we are all in the bedroom, and Sapphire jumps up onto the bed, gingerly pulling back the sheets with her teeth, then helping Baxter roll Tess onto the bed, before positioning her so that she looks like she's sleeping, her head resting on the dust coated pillow. As soon as this is done, Sapphire covers her with the thin covers, so that all you can see is a bump where her thin body lies and the tip of her nose peeking out above the sheets. Sapphire then returns to Ruby, who is standing with Sophia, as I start a sort of speech.

"Tess," I start, a lump forming in my throat that I try hard to swallow down, "Was the best of dogs. A kind and loyal creature, I cannot think of a finer dog. She was the best of her kind, calm and collected at all times, and I cannot imagine how our lives would have turned out without her. She will be dearly missed, by all of us."

Sophia is crying quietly, Ruby comforting her, as Baxter steps forwards, as if addressing Tess herself.

"Ma, you were the greatest dog there ever was. Better than me, better than all them strays, better than any dog there ever was. We should all be like you, so clever and reasonable, but we aren't, and I wish we were. You made the world a better place, ma, and I miss you. A lot. Please say you're watching over me, up in the sky."

He stops, eyes shut, and the room falls into a respectful silence for about a minute, until Ruby takes Sophia downstairs, Sapphire close behind, and it's just me and Baxter. But, after thirty seconds, I decide to leave him and his thoughts alone, so I head back downstairs and curl up on the Armchair with the Twins and Sophia, watching T.V. But my mind isn't focused on the programme. Thoughts flitter around my head like butterflies, mostly around the subject of people leaving us. First Joseph, but he could come back, and now Tess, who can't come back. Who's next? Do I even want to know?

Chapter Fifteen

Life without Tess is almost unbearable. Baxter hangs his head low every day, all his childish enthusiasm and excitement long gone. Everyone is hungry, again, but this time there is no miracle answer to save us. Sophia's nightmares are worse, so all of us cats sleep on the Armchair together. One night, Ruby (Yes, Ruby, who usually hates the very scent of that dog) even invited Baxter to sleep with us, so now he gets on the Armchair first, and we curl up around him.

It's also getting colder, but if that's because we have no food, and therefore less body fat to keep us warm, or if it's just because it's getting colder outside I don't know. It could be both. It could be neither. We don't seem to know anything for certain now. I don't even know what day it is, as the T.V has stopped working. One day, we tried to turn it on, and it just refused to come to life. That was a sad day.

The radiator has also stopped working, which is probably another reason why Baxter comes over to sleep with us. With Tess gone, it feels like there is always something - or rather, someone - missing. The place where she slept every night is now always empty, but I still glance there every morning, as if to wake up the dog who can never be woken. Not anymore. Our lives are incomplete without Tess being here to guide us.

Every so often, I'll look at the window and wonder what it would be like to be out there. Have things changed since I stalked the streets? Are the strays different now? I doubt it. Strays will always be the same, miserable and violent. Few have ever changed, but I am lucky enough to be one of those few. Unfortunately, that leaves hundreds of other strays to carry on being miserable and violent, and I doubt they'll ever change.

As I look around at my Tribe, I am filled with sadness. Their faces all bear the same look, one of hunger and despair. No hope anymore, oh no, that's all gone now. Four days without Tess did that to us. Four whole days. Not a week, but it's long enough. I just wish everything could go right for once. I wish we could find food, good food, and survive for just a bit longer. But it won't happen. Because this is real life, and life is hard. I learnt that a long time ago, but it's meaning was lost in the years that I had

Joseph to look after me. I suppose this is just life's cruel way of reminding me.

Today, all we have to look forward to is the possibility of rats, if we're lucky, or old cat-food, if we're extremely lucky, for dinner. That's it. The rest of the day is just planned out to be searching for food, then having a rest, then searching for more food, then waiting for Sapphire and Ruby to finish hunting, then searching for food once more before going to sleep. It's not like we want our lives to be boring and bleak, but there's nothing else to do. We're just never in the right mood to play, or make jokes, or even talk sometimes.

I start to look for food in the cupboards, like I do everyday, but not even the faintest scent of food remains. Looking round, I can see Baxter desperately digging through piles of rubbish, but never finding anything edible. Ruby and Sapphire are having even less luck over in the Living-Room, as almost all the rats and mice seem to have vanished, leaving us with nothing to eat. Sophia is sleeping on the Armchair, a blanket covering her frail body. If we do find any food, she's definitely eating first. I can't bear to think about Sophia starving, but it is happening.

We're all slowly starving, and there's nothing I can do about it, except look for more food, which is proving itself to be both a terrible and useless idea.

We're all quite thin, but I think it shows on Sophia the most. I know she's not exactly a kitten anymore, but she is still very small. The smallest in her litter, if I remember correctly. I suppose the absence of food that isn't extremely old or almost inedible in her diet doesn't really help, but I wish I could do something. Anything. It's torture, having to watch the cats (And dog) that you consider to be family just dying away, slowly. Baxter's childish excitement and joy has all but gone, and Ruby doesn't even bother arguing with him anymore. Sapphire doesn't speak at all, except the odd word that is whispered in Ruby's ear, and Sophia stays close to me all the time, barely leaving my side. The only time that she is on her own is in the early morning, like now, when we all start looking for food and leave her to get a couple more hours of sleep.

Sleep. It's like a short distraction to what's going on in the real world. Well, when you have dreams. When I have those dreamless nights, usually when we've found nothing to eat at all and it's really cold, sleep serves less like a distraction and more like a blindfold. But, when the blindfold is taken off, it's back to the cruel reality that is our lives, and it's always disappointing. I mean, when you think about it, things could be worse. We could have to deal with the chilling winds from outside, and the horrendous rain, or even hail sometimes. But we don't, because we're in a house, where everything is dry but cold and sheltered but lonely. It's a hard choice, you have to admit. It's either being drenched and freezing on the streets or desolate and freezing in a house. And I'm not sure which I prefer.

Of course, I know immediately which life I like best, before or after being adopted. After, of course. If I hadn't been adopted then I wouldn't have met Ruby, Sapphire, Tess or Baxter, although I would have still have known Sophia, or at least seen her. If Joseph hadn't taken me in, then I would be lonely. It's true. I used to always steer clear of relationships or even friendships with other cats, only ever meeting them when a fight was going to occur, and I was going to be in that fight. Dogs? Don't even get me started. I would never have talked to a dog, ever. I always thought that they were filthy, stupid animals, and that the only thing they were even relatively good at was fighting. And while that might've been true for the dogs I was talking about at the time, the dirty strays that roamed the back alleys of the city after dark, I now know that not all dogs are like that. Some are like Baxter, or at least like how Baxter used to be. Childish, excitable, and extremely gullible. I would even go as far as saying he's the tiniest bit stupid. Just a tiny bit. And then there's dogs like Tess. Kind, loyal, brave and clever. There wasn't one bad bone in Tess' entire body. And I respected her for that. I still respect her.

We've got to do something, though, and soon. Time is running out and, if I don't do something soon, we could die in here. I know I've said that we could starve before, but I'm saying it again, for a reason. It's a fact.

"Shadow!" My head quickly turns in the direction of the voice, and I am surprised to see Ruby coming into the Kitchen.

"Yes?"

"We've got a rat. Sapphire caught it. Best one we've seen in days. It's also the first one we've seen in days. Sapphire wants Sophia to have the first bit, but then it's up to you." Her voice isn't exactly bursting with enthusiasm, but I know from the look on her face that she's really excited.

"Good. You wake up Sophia, I'll get Baxter."

She nods at me, before bounding into the Living-Room. I turn to Baxter, who has already heard the conversation, but I tell him the news anyway. He gives me a weak smile, before heading into the Living-Room. I follow him, shutting the cupboard behind me and quickening my step as I enter the Living-Room. Sophia is being woken up by Ruby, and she speeds over to me when she sees me come in, the smallest of smiles on her face, her eyes gleaming with happiness. I smile back, feeling truly happy for once, before turning to Sapphire and the medium sized brown rat beside her. The smell is beautiful, if a smell can even be beautiful, and it is just inviting me to tear it apart and eat it all, but I restrain myself. Sophia must eat first.

Sapphire nods at me, as I step forwards and use my claws to cut a generous piece out for Sophia, who is positively beaming as she bites into it, purring. We all chuckle, even Baxter, before eating our own bits. Baxter even manages to produce some ancient cat biscuits, which smell awful and taste worse, but we eat them anyway, thankful of something to fill our stomachs.

As we all lie down on the Armchair, preparing to rest before going to search for food again, Baxter nudges me, asking if he can make an announcement. I am confused, very confused, but I agree anyway, and he clears his throat. Sapphire stops murmuring to Ruby and they both focus their attention on him, Sophia too. I search his face for clues as to what he is going to say, but come up empty, so I just wait. Finally, he starts to speak. And I am astounded by what he says.

"I think..." He hesitates for a moment, before continuing, "I think we should get out of here. Joseph's not going to come back. Not now, not ever."

Lightning Source UK Ltd.
Milton Keynes UK
UKHW021927270519
343407UK00001B/14/P

9 781364 980634